"You, however, my sweet darling Holly, heated my blood from the first moment I saw you."

He cupped her face and bent down to kiss her.

Not a hard kiss. Or a hungry one. A soft, tender, loving kiss that rocked her soul.

What a fool she was. A silly fool. Didn't she know she'd been half in love with him before she even met him? He was everything she'd ever wanted in a man. The trouble was, as perfect as he was in her eyes, in his heart of hearts, he would always belong to someone else.

Tears pricked at her eyes, bringing panic. She didn't want him to know how she felt about him. He might use the knowledge against her. Make her do things she knew she shouldn't do, like say yes to marrying him.

When a wealthy man wants a wife, he doesn't always follow the rules!

Welcome to Miranda Lee's stunning,
sexy new trilogy—
Meet Richard, Reece and Mike, three Sydney millionaires with a mission—they all want to get married...but none wants to fall in love!

Bought: One Bride
Richard's story:
**His money can buy him anything he wants...
and he wants a wife!**
August 2005
2483

The Tycoon's Trophy Wife
Reece's story:
**She was everything he wanted in a wife...
'til he fell in love with her!**
September 2005
#2489

A Scandalous Marriage
Mike's story:
**He married her for money—
her beauty was a bonus!**
October 2005
#2496

Miranda Lee

BOUGHT: ONE BRIDE

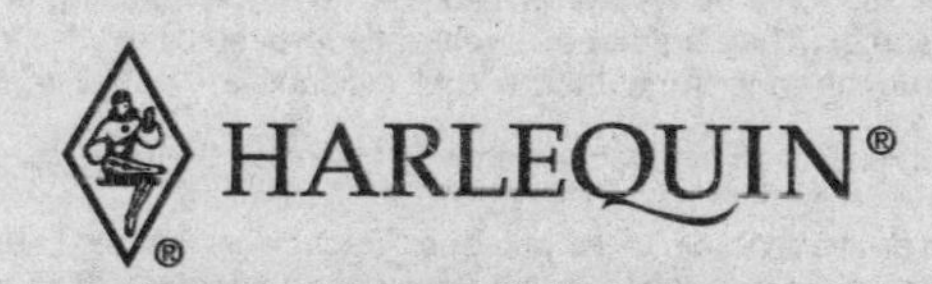

TORONTO • NEW YORK • LONDON
AMSTERDAM • PARIS • SYDNEY • HAMBURG
STOCKHOLM • ATHENS • TOKYO • MILAN • MADRID
PRAGUE • WARSAW • BUDAPEST • AUCKLAND

ISBN 0-373-12483-X

BOUGHT: ONE BRIDE

First North American Publication 2005.

This edition published by arrangement with Harlequin Books S.A.

www.eHarlequin.com

Printed in U.S.A.

PROLOGUE

THE lift purred its way up to the penthouse floor, coming to a quiet halt before the door slid smoothly open, revealing a marble-floored foyer underfoot, and a breathtaking view straight ahead. Sydney Harbour on a clear summer's day was always a sight to behold, with its sparkling blue water and picturesque surrounds, but more so from this height and this vantage point.

Richard shook his head as he walked from the lift towards the huge plate-glass window, his expression wry as he glanced over his shoulder at Reece, who'd hung back a little.

"I can see why you've had no trouble selling these apartments," he remarked to his friend and business colleague. "I've never seen a finer view."

Reece's handsome face showed satisfaction as he came forward to stand at Richard's shoulder. "I always abide by that famous old real estate saying. Position. Position. Position. Aside from being north-facing with a great view of the bridge, this point at East Balmain is just a short ferry ride from Sydney's Central Business District, and an even shorter ride across to Darling Harbour."

"It's certainly a top spot, especially being near to the CBD. Which is just as well," Richard added. "There were mutterings at the bank all last year that I'd used their money to back one too many of your projects. My new position as CEO could have been on the line if this had proved to be one big white elephant. The board were seriously worried when you wouldn't allow investors to buy off the plan.''

Reece smiled. ''Aah, but these apartments weren't directed at investors. They were designed so that people would fall in love with at least one of them and want to live here. As well as devoting two floors to a private gym, pool, sauna and squash courts, I had each apartment individually decorated and furnished, right down to the sheets, towels and accessories. It added between one and two hundred thousand to the cost of each apartment, but it's proved to be a most successful selling tool.''

Richard winced. Up to two hundred thousand, spent decorating each apartment. Good God.

''I'm glad you didn't tell me that earlier. The old fogies at the bank would have had a pink fit. I might have too,'' he added with a dry laugh. There were factions at the bank who didn't approve of Richard's promotion last year. A couple of the senior executives thought he was too young at thirty-eight to run a multibillion-dollar financial institution.

''That's why I didn't tell you till now,'' Reece said with a wry grin. ''I know when to keep a secret. But you've had the last laugh, dear friend,'' he said, clapping Richard on the shoulder. ''The building's only been open since last October and we already have a ninety-five per cent occupancy rate. Three short months, and there's only one penthouse left empty, along with a few apartments on the lower floors.''

''What's wrong with the penthouse you haven't

sold?'' Richard asked. ''Too expensive? Wrong colour scheme?''

''Nope. It's not on the market.''

''Aah. The developer has claimed it for himself.''

Reece's blue eyes twinkled. ''Come on. I'll show it to you.''

''I can understand now why you've kept this one,'' Richard said ten minutes later.

It was nothing like other city penthouses Richard had seen during his lifetime. And he'd seen quite a few. This was like a house up in the sky. A beach house, complete with garden beds, a lap pool and wide, cream-tiled terraces where you could stretch out and enjoy the view and soak up the sun.

Inside, the décor continued the promise of a relaxed, sun-filled lifestyle, with the same cream tiles on the floors throughout. The walls were painted either cream or a warm buttery colour. Most of the furniture was made of natural cane, with soft furnishings in various shades of blue. Rugs in blues and yellows gave warmth to the tiled floors.

No curtains or blinds blocked the view, though the glass doors and windows were tinted to reduce any glare. Naturally, the interior was fully air-conditioned and Reece proudly announced there was heating under the floor tiles to warm the place in the winter. Every room had a view and sliding glass doors that led out onto the terraces. A high cement wall separated the two top-floor penthouses, providing privacy and a courtyard effect to house the lap pool.

When Richard walked into the spacious master bedroom with its luxuriously large bed and built-in television screen in the wall opposite, a feeling of sheer envy consumed him.

He'd always admired Reece for his tenacity and resilience, admired how he'd picked himself up both professionally and personally a few years back and worked his way back from the brink of bankruptcy to his current position as the golden boy of Sydney's property development business.

But he had never, ever envied him.

Till now.

Suddenly, Richard wanted this penthouse. Wanted to live in it. Wanted to come home to it every night, instead of the cold, soulless apartment he'd occupied since his wife's death eighteen months ago. He even wanted to share it with someone, which was a surprise as well. Up till this moment, the thought of sharing his life—and his bed—with another woman had been anathema to him. He'd been in total emotional shutdown since he'd buried Joanna. Total sexual shutdown as well.

No wonder he'd been capable of putting in twenty-four-hour days at the bank. His male hormones had to be directed somewhere. It seemed, however, that his male hormones were about to emerge from their cryogenic state, for when Richard looked at the king-sized bed in front of his eyes, he didn't envisage sleeping in it alone.

His flesh actually stirred with the mental image of himself making love to a woman on top of that blue satin quilt. No one he already knew. An attractive stranger. Brunette. Soft-eyed. Full-breasted. And very willing.

His flesh stirred even further.

"You really like this place, don't you?" Reece said.

Richard laughed. "I didn't think I was that obvious. But, yes, I really do. Would you consider selling it to me?"

"Nope."

Frustration flared within Richard, alongside another surge of testosterone. "Damn it, Reece, you already own a mansion on the water just around the corner. What do you want this place for?"

"To give to you."

"What?" Richard's eyebrows shot ceiling-wards.

Reece smiled that disarming, charming smile of his. "Here are the keys, my friend. It's yours."

"Don't be ridiculous!" Richard exclaimed, though his heart was hammering inside his chest. "I can't let you do that. Hell, this place has to be worth a small fortune."

"Five point four million the other penthouse sold for, to be precise. But this one is bigger and better. Here." And he pressed the keys into Richard's right hand.

"No, no. You *have* to let me pay for it!"

"Absolutely not. It's all yours, in appreciation. You were there for me, Rich, when no one else was. And I'm not just talking about the money. You gave me your hand in friendship. And you had faith in my judgement. That's worth more than all the money in the world."

Richard didn't know what to say. Only twice in his banking career had he made personal friends of men he'd lent money to. It was generally advised against. But he'd never had any cause to regret either decision.

Reece, of course, was always a hard man to say no to, and impossible not to like.

Mike had been a different kettle of fish entirely. As dark in looks and personality as Reece was light and bright, the young computer genius had come to the bank several years ago for backing to start his own software company. A one-time juvenile delinquent who had a permanent chip on his shoulder, Mike had no ability to sell himself at all.

But he was creatively brilliant, cripplingly honest and unashamedly ambitious. Richard had been so impressed, he'd invested his own money into Mike's company as well as the bank's.

Over time, Richard had found himself really liking Mike as well, despite his gruff manner. He'd persuaded Mike to go along to one of Reece's famous parties and the three of them had soon become close friends.

Nowadays, Richard counted Reece and Mike as his best and only true friends. Other male colleagues in his life pretended friendship, but Richard knew that they had knives ready behind his back, to be used if he gave them a chance.

"You have no idea how much this means to me," Richard said, his hand closing tightly around the keys. "But to accept a luxury penthouse as a gift—especially *this* one—would put me in an impossible position at the bank. My enemies would have a field day. There'd be all sorts of rumours about corruption and paybacks and Lord knows what else. You *must* let me pay for it."

"You and that bloody bank and those pompous pricks you work with!"

Richard laughed. ''Yes, I know, but it's *my* bloody bank now and I'd like to keep it that way. I'll give you the proper market value. What would that be? Six million?''

''Probably.'' Reece sighed. ''Very well. Six million.''

''Look, it's not as though I can't afford it,'' Richard pointed out. ''I made a packet out of the house at Palm Beach I bought.'' And which he'd sold a week after Joanna's funeral.

Richard didn't add that in the eighteen months since Joanna's death, he'd also tripled his personal fortune in the stock market. Amazing what profits could be made when you were uncaring of the risks you were taking.

He could retire right now on his portfolio of property and shares.

But of course he wouldn't. He enjoyed the cut and thrust of the financial world; enjoyed the power of his new position, and the prestige that went with it.

Richard wondered momentarily what Joanna would have made of his success, if she'd still been alive. She would have liked the money, and the social life his new job required of him. But would it have kept her solely in his bed?

Richard doubted it. Any woman who took a lover within two years of her marriage had to be unfaithful by nature.

If it hadn't been for the autopsy report, he would never have known the awful truth about the woman he loved. He'd questioned the coroner at length about the age of the child Joanna had been carrying when the car accident had claimed her life, but he'd been told there was no mistake. Six weeks, give or take a few days.

Richard had been overseas on business for over a month surrounding the time of conception.

The child was not his.

Richard's hand closed even more tightly around the keys. He'd wanted a child with her so much. But Joanna had kept putting him off, saying she wasn't ready for dirty nappies and sleepless nights.

The thing that tormented him the most—now that he could bear to think about it—was the way she'd greeted him when he'd returned home that last time. As if she'd truly loved him. As if she'd missed him so much. She hadn't been able to get enough of him in bed, when all the while she'd been carrying another man's child.

Clearly, she'd been going to pass the baby off as his.

What kind of woman could do that?

Richard had buried both of them with a broken heart, then buried himself in his career.

They said time healed everything. Perhaps so. But Richard knew his life would never be the same, post-Joanna. He could never fall in love again for starters. That part of him had died with her.

But he didn't want to continue living alone.

And he still wanted a child.

It was definitely time to move on. Time to find himself a new wife, the way Reece had found Alanna after his fiancée had dumped him.

''You have that look on your face,'' Reece said, breaking the silence in the bedroom.

''What look is that?''

"The one you get when you're about to ask me endless questions, usually on the new project I've just come to you with."

The corner of Richard's mouth twitched. "You're a remarkably intuitive man. I do have some questions for you. And, yes, it's about a project of yours. But not a new one. One you completed last year. Shall we go out onto the terrace and sit down?"

"I've never known you to be so mysterious," he said as he followed Richard through the sliding glass doors out into the sunshine.

Richard pulled out one of the chairs of the nearest outdoor setting and sat down. There were several arrangements dotted around the various terraces. This was made in cream aluminium, with a glass-topped table and pale blue, all-weather cushions on the chairs.

Richard waited till Reece was settled opposite him before he spoke.

"I've decided I want to get married again," he began.

"But that's great!" his friend proclaimed. "I didn't realise you were seeing someone."

"I'm not. But I hope to be soon, once you put me in touch with the woman who runs Wives Wanted."

Reece's mouth dropped open before snapping shut again. "But you didn't approve when I told you about that."

"I was surprised, that's all." A reasonable reaction, in Richard's opinion. Reece was not the sort of man one would ever imagine using an introduction agency. His confession to his best man and groomsman just before his wedding last year that he'd found his beautiful new bride via an internet website had come as a shock.

The agency was called Wives Wanted, its aim being to match professional men with the kind of women lots of them wanted to marry, especially those of the "once bitten, twice shy" brigade. Apparently, its database was chock-full of attractive women who were only interested in one career. Marriage. Women whose priority was not necessarily romantic love, but security and commitment.

A lot of them had had previous marriages, or relationships, that had failed to deliver what they wanted in life. Some were currently career girls, but were prepared to relegate their careers to the back seat, for the right man.

"It was Mike who didn't approve," Richard pointed out. "But don't forget, he hadn't met Alanna at that stage."

Thankfully, Richard had stopped Mike from repeating to Reece at the reception that he thought all women who put themselves out like that were nothing but cold-blooded gold-diggers, looking for a gravy train to ride. He'd voiced that opinion to Richard, however. More than once.

But no one who got to know Reece's wife would believe such a thing of her.

Richard had initially been stunned when Reece had confessed that he'd found his lovely Alanna through this agency. He'd presumed Reece had met her socially. After all, he had a very active social life. A man of his looks and position could have had his pick of women.

When Richard had asked him outright at the wedding reception why he'd gone to an introduction agency, Reece's reply had been very to the point, and extremely pragmatic.

"It was a question of time. I wanted a wife and a family, but I didn't want to be bothered with a traditional courtship. Far too lengthy a process. Whenever I want a property with certain requirements, I get my PA to narrow the field down for me before I look personally. I approached finding a wife the same way. I gave Wives Wanted a list of my requirements and they selected several suitable candidates for me to view via the internet. I chose three who appealed to me. I only had to date each one once and I knew straight away which girl I would marry."

Richard recalled naïvely asking Reece if it was a case of love at first sight, at which Mike had laughed.

"Reece isn't interested in love any more," Mike had drily informed him. "Not after that other bitch did the dirty on him. Isn't that right, Reece?"

Reece had confirmed that love certainly hadn't come into the equation, on either side, although he claimed he wouldn't have married Alanna without some sexual chemistry between them.

Some sexual chemistry?

Richard still considered this a rather outrageous understatement. He'd had several opportunities to observe Reece and Alanna together, both before and after their wedding. To his eyes, the sexual chemistry between them was quite electric, especially on Reece's part.

Richard had noted at a recent dinner party he'd attended at the Diamonds' place that Reece had spent an inordinate amount of time watching his beautiful wife talking to the male guest sitting next to her.

Admittedly, Alanna had looked extra stunning that night in a clinging white satin gown that made the most of her physical assets. There hadn't been a man sitting at that table who hadn't found his eyes coming back to her all the time, himself included.

Richard thought it was just as well that ethereal-looking blondes with porcelain skin, pale green eyes and tall, willowy figures didn't overly stir his male hormones. He preferred the more earthy kind of women, with stronger colouring and lush bodies.

Joanna had had black hair, black eyes and a voluptuous figure.

Not that Richard wanted to marry some clone of Joanna. Hell, no. He wanted the second Mrs Richard Crawford to be as far removed from the first as a woman could be. In personality and character, that was. Physically, he'd always been attracted to brunettes with curves. He knew, when he eventually studied the Wives Wanted database, he wouldn't be selecting any skinny blondes.

"Are you absolutely sure about this?" Reece asked him.

"Absolutely."

"I presume you're not looking for love, then."

"You presume correctly."

"You want a marriage of convenience. Like mine."

"Yes."

Reece frowned. "I'm not sure you're cut out for a relationship like that, Rich. You're a bit of a romantic at heart."

"Not any more, I'm not."

Richard wished he hadn't sounded quite so bitter. Reece looked startled. As well he might. Reece knew nothing about Joanna's betrayal. Men, even the closest of friends, didn't tell each other things like that.

"I've made up my mind about this," Richard stated firmly.

"Can I ask why?" Reece probed.

"It's not rocket science, my friend. Just the need for companionship. And some regular sex."

"You could get that from a girlfriend."

"I don't want a girlfriend. I want a wife."

"Aah, I get the picture. It's because of the bank. Your position as CEO would be consolidated if you were married."

Now it was Richard's turn to be startled. "It has nothing whatsoever to do with the bank. I simply want to be married. I want what you've got, Reece. A good-looking woman who's happy to be my wife, and to have my child."

"I didn't realise you wanted a family."

"Why on earth would you think that?"

Reece shrugged. "You were married to Joanna for two years, more than enough time to have a baby."

"That was not my doing," Richard informed his friend, doing his best not to sound cold.

Reece still frowned. "I thought you were happy with Joanna..."

"I was," he said truthfully enough. His unhappiness hadn't begun till after she'd died. "I was mad about her. But she's gone, and I'm here and I'm lonely, all right? I want a woman in my life. What I don't want, however, is romance. I've been there, done that.''

Reece nodded. ''Yes, I can understand where you're coming from.''

''You should. I know how you felt about Kristine. Which is why *you* went to Wives Wanted in the first place. Because you were still in love with her.''

''The way you still are with Joanna.''

Richard didn't deny it. If he had, he might have had to explain.

''Now that that's all settled, I'm going back inside to have another look at my fabulous new penthouse,'' he said, scraping back his chair and standing up. ''Which reminds me. Can I move in before contracts are exchanged?''

''Move in today, if you like.''

Richard was not an impulsive man by nature but, today, things were a-changing. ''You know what? I think I will.''

CHAPTER ONE

HOLLY glared for the umpteenth time at the FOR SALE sign that had been taped on the shop window less than half an hour earlier. Fury and indignation warred inside her swirling stomach and whirling head.

How dared her stepmother do this? How *dared* she?

A Flower A Day was at least half hers by rights. She should have been consulted. Should have been considered.

But any consideration for *her* feelings had clearly ended with her father's death. Any hope of his beloved business one day being hers had died with him.

She'd been stupid to stay on. Especially stupid to work for such a pathetic salary, considering she managed the shop now, and did the books as well. Every Sunday, no less. Her day off!

Heck, Sara took home almost as much money as she did. And Sara only worked from Wednesday till Saturday as a casual. Sure, Sara was an excellent florist with loads of experience but Holly was every bit as experienced. She might only be twenty-six but she'd been working with flowers all her life. Her dad had started training her to be a florist when she'd been knee-high to a grasshopper. She'd joined him in the shop soon after her fifteenth birthday.

Holly's heart twisted as she remembered how happy they'd been back then. Just her and her dad.

And then Connie had come along.

Holly hadn't realised till after her dad had died two years back what kind of woman her stepmother was. Connie had been very clever during the eight years she'd been the second Mrs Greenaway.

But Holly had certainly known within weeks of her dad marrying the attractive divorcee that her stepsister was a nasty piece of work. Jealous, spiteful and devious. Unfortunately, Katie had been equally clever with her new stepfather as his new wife had.

Butter wouldn't melt in her mouth around him.

Holly bitterly resented the money Connie and Katie had wheedled out of her dad. Only the fact that he'd seemed happy had made her stay silent over the vicious things Katie had said to her in private.

Of course, after her dad had died, all gloves had been off. Connie had begun showing her true colours and Katie…well, Katie had gone from bad to worse.

Holly knew she should have moved out of their lives altogether right then and there, but she just couldn't bear to part company with her dad's flower shop. She still felt close to him there. So she'd moved into the flat above the shop and set about getting A Flower A Day back on track.

Business had fallen right off after her father's stroke, Holly having been so upset that she'd had to close the shop for a while. It had taken over a year to get all his old clients back and to start making a profit. Not that A Flower A Day would ever be a great money-making concern. Strip shopping wasn't very successful these days. The malls had taken over.

The shop and the flat, however, were still worth good money, despite being ancient and not in the best of condition. Probably over a million. More if someone bought it as a business, along with the goodwill.

Holly glowered at the FOR SALE sign one more time. She'd been crazy to work so hard for so little when she'd known, deep down, that the only ones who would reap the rewards were Connie and the obnoxious Katie. Unfortunately, her father had left his wife everything in his will, made soon after they'd been married when Holly had only been sixteen. He'd relied on Connie to look after his daughter. But the merry widow had had other plans.

So had her rotten daughter…

But Holly didn't want to think about that. She'd thought about what had happened over Christmas far too much already.

If Dave had really loved her, Katie would not have been able to steal him. But she had. She was even going to marry him. That should have been the final straw for Holly but, strangely enough, it hadn't been.

The final straw was that FOR SALE sign.

Holly decided then and there that she'd played Cinderella long enough. The time had come for some major changes and major decisions. She knew she'd be very sad to walk away from her dad's pride and joy, but it had to be done. Because it wasn't going to be *her* pride and joy for much longer. It would soon belong to someone else.

"I'm just ducking down to the station, Sara," she said crisply. "I need this morning's *Herald*."

Sara glanced up from where she was finishing an exquisite table setting of pink carnations. It was for a local lady who was a pink addict.

"Looking for a new job?" Sara said.

"Absolutely."

"About time," Sara muttered.

A very attractive redhead in her midthirties, Sara had seen plenty of living and did not suffer fools gladly. She'd long expressed the opinion that Holly should strike out on her own.

"You're right," Holly agreed. "I'll be looking for a new place to live as well."

Sydney's Saturday morning *Herald* was always chock-full of job and flat-share advertisements. Holly had actually looked before; a few weeks ago, after Dave had left her for Katie. She just hadn't had the courage at that stage to totally change her life, and to leave everything that was so familiar to her.

But she'd found the courage now.

Sara smiled her approval. "Atta girl. And don't you go worrying about me. As soon as you're out of here, so am I. I wouldn't work for that cow Connie if this was the last flower shop in Sydney."

"She is a cow, isn't she?"

"Of the highest order. And so's the daughter. For what it's worth, Katie deserves Dave. I was pleased as Punch the day you got rid of him."

"Er...he dumped me, Sara."

"Only good thing he ever did for you. Now you can find yourself a really nice bloke, someone who'll appreciate your qualities."

"Thanks for the compliment, Sara, but really nice blokes are hard to find. They certainly haven't been thick on the ground in my life. Dave's not the first loser boyfriend I've had. I seem to attract the fickle, faithless type."

"Go get yourself a job in the city, love. Where the suits are."

"Suits?"

"You know. Men in suits. Executive types. I used to work at a flower stall in Market Place. There was an endless parade of male eye candy walking by there, I can tell you. Talk about yummy."

"Yes, but does wearing a suit to work equate with being a nice bloke?"

"Nope. But it often equates with money. Might as well fall for a rich guy as a poor guy."

"*You* didn't." Sara was married to a man who worked on the railways.

"Yes, well, I'm a romantic fool."

"I'm a romantic fool as well."

Sara pulled a face. "Yeah. Most of us girls are. Oh well, you'd better go get that *Herald* before they're all gone."

Holly bought the last paper in the newsagent's and hurried back to study the classifieds between customers, but the news was disappointing. There weren't very many jobs for florists advertised that weekend. And only two in the city. As for sharing a flat…

The reality of moving in with strangers after living on her own for two years made Holly shudder. Yet she couldn't afford to rent somewhere decent by herself, not unless her salary was pretty good. She certainly couldn't afford to buy a place. She had *some* savings but not much. A couple of thousand. Having Dave as a boyfriend had not been cheap. She'd ended up paying for most things, his excuse being he was saving up for their future together.

Like, how gullible could a girl get?

Facing her shortcomings was not a pleasant experience. But by the time Sara left to go home at four o'clock and Holly began closing up the shop, she'd come to terms with her own pathetic performance as a supposedly adult woman. She had no one to blame but herself if her life was a shambles. She'd taken the line of least resistance and allowed people to walk all over her.

But no more. Come Monday morning she would get in contact with one of the many services who did professional résumés. She'd never had to apply for a job before but she knew you had to present yourself well. Then she would apply for those two jobs in the city. Sara was right. The city was the way to go.

But she wasn't going to fall into the trap of accepting any job that paid poorly. She would need a good salary if she wanted to keep living by herself.

She didn't have to rush. Businesses like A Flower A Day did not sell overnight. She probably had a couple of months at least to make her plans and execute them.

Meanwhile, she wasn't going to breathe a word to Connie. And she would stash away every cent she could.

The sight of a huge bunch of red roses sitting in a bucket in the corner brought Holly up with a jolt. It was a phone order she had taken yesterday afternoon. Not one of her usual clients. A man, who'd promised to pick them up by noon today.

With a sigh, she checked her records, found his name and number, and rang.

An answering machine. Botheration. She hated answering machines.

After leaving a message saying she'd cancelled the order, Holly hung up with a sigh.

What a waste. Such lovely red roses. Expensive, too. He hadn't wanted buds, but open flowers. They wouldn't last more than a few days. Impossible to sell them to anyone else.

And then an idea came to her.

Mrs Crawford. She absolutely loved roses, and she wasn't due to leave on her overseas jaunt till the end of next week. Holly could call them a going-away gift. Plus a thank you for all the times she'd dropped into the shop for a chat and a cuppa.

Nice woman, Mrs Crawford.

If Holly's thoughts drifted momentarily to Richard Crawford, she didn't allow them to linger. Yet there was a time when she'd thought about Mrs Crawford's precious only son quite a bit. She'd even woven wild fantasies around him, about their meeting one day and his being bowled over by her.

Sara was right. Most women were romantic fools!

Flicking her address book over to the Cs, she checked Mrs Crawford's number and rang to make sure she'd be there.

Engaged.

Oh, well, at least she was home.

Holly bent to scoop the roses out of the bucket, wrapped them in some silver paper and tied them with a red bow the same colour as the blooms. She would walk up to Mrs Crawford's house and give them to her personally. It wasn't far and the day was still pleasantly warm. The sun didn't set till late and it was only four-fifteen.

When Holly set out, it never occurred to her that

Richard Crawford might be at his mother's house, even if it *was* the weekend. Mrs Crawford had told her just the other day that she rarely saw her son any more. Apparently, he'd been promoted to CEO at his bank—the youngest ever!—and was more of a workaholic than ever.

Holly took her time, strolling rather than striding out, enjoying the fresh air and mentally running through her list of things to do in the coming weeks.

Number one. Find a job, preferably in the city.

Number two. Find a flat, preferably near the city.

Number three. Find herself a nice bloke. Preferably one who wore a suit and worked in the city.

Holly pulled a face, then struck number three off her list. That could definitely wait a while.

Regardless of how much of a two-timing rat Dave had turned out to be, he'd still been her boyfriend for over a year and she'd thought she loved him. Had thought he loved her as well. He'd said he did often enough.

Dave's dumping her for Katie had really hurt. Holly's self-esteem was still seriously bruised and she simply wasn't ready to launch herself back into the dating scene.

No, she would concentrate on the two things she could manage. A new job and a new place to live.

Finding a new boyfriend was not on her agenda, not for quite some time.

CHAPTER TWO

"I'M GOING now."

Richard looked up from his laptop, taking a few moments to focus on his mother, who was standing in the study doorway.

"You're looking very smart," he said.

"Thank you," she returned, her hand lifting to lightly touch her exquisitely groomed blonde hair. "Nice of you to notice."

Richard had noticed more than her new hair. She was a totally different woman today, all due to Melvin's arrival in her life, no doubt.

"I'm sorry I'm going out, Richard. But you could have warned me you were dropping by. I haven't seen hide nor hair of you for weeks."

"I've been exceptionally busy," he said, and let her think he meant at the bank.

In reality, he'd been busy, wining and dining his five final selections from Wives Wanted. So far he'd taken out four of them. The first three, on successive Saturday nights. Number four, however, hadn't been able to make it tonight, so he'd taken her out last night.

The evening had proved as disappointing as the three previous dinner dates.

Richard had been going to go into work today—he often worked on a Saturday—but he'd decided at the last moment, and in a spirit of total exasperation, to come and tell his mother about his quest for a new wife via Wives Wanted. He hadn't wanted to discuss his lack of success so far with Reece, and certainly not with Mike, who knew nothing of his wife-finding endeavours. Richard had even brought his laptop with him to show his mother the Wives Wanted database.

But when he'd arrived she'd been so excited about her own date with Melvin that Richard had abandoned that idea.

And now he was glad he had. Because she would never understand why he wanted a marriage of convenience. Not unless he told her the truth about Joanna. And he refused to bare his soul like that.

"I won't be back till late," she said. "We're going to the theatre after dinner. But there's pizza in the freezer. And a nice bottle of wine in the door of the fridge."

"Watch it, Mum. You're in danger of becoming a party girl."

Her face visibly stiffened. "And what if I am?" she snapped. "I think it's about time, don't you?"

Richard was startled by her reaction. Did she think he was criticising her?

Possibly. His father had been a critical bastard. He didn't know how his mother had stood being married to him. It had been bad enough being his son. Richard had learned to survive by excelling in all his endeavours. Difficult for a father to find fault when his son came first at everything.

After his father had died several years back, Richard had expected his mother to marry again. She'd only been in her late fifties at the time. And she was a good-looking woman. Reginald Crawford wouldn't have married any other kind.

But she hadn't married again. She'd lived a very quiet life, playing bowls once a week on ladies day, and bridge on a Tuesday night. Mostly, she stayed at home where she looked after her garden, watched TV and read. Then suddenly, at sixty-five, the travel bug had hit.

Not wanting to explore the world alone, she'd placed an ad on the community bulletin board at the local library for a travelling companion. Melvin had applied a fortnight ago and was found to be very agreeable. A retired surgeon, he was a widower as well. Not a man to let grass grow under his feet, Melvin had already organised their world trip to start this coming Friday.

''I wasn't being critical, Mum,'' Richard said carefully. ''I think what you're doing is fabulous.''

''You mean that, Richard? You don't think I'm being foolish?''

''Not at all. But I would like to meet Melvin personally before you leave.''

''Check up on him, you mean.''

''You are quite a wealthy widow, Mum,'' he pointed out. ''And I'm your only son. I have to keep an eye on my future inheritance, you know.''

This was a load of garbage and his mother knew it. Richard had made more money during his relatively short banking career than his father had in forty years of accounting. Reginald Crawford had always been too conservative with his own investments. He gave excellent advice to his clients but couldn't seem to transfer that to his own portfolio.

Still, by the time he'd dropped dead of a heart attack at the age of seventy, he'd been able to leave his wife their Strathfield home, mortgage-free, along with a superannuation policy that would keep her in comfort till her own death. Which hopefully wouldn't be for many years to come.

"You don't have to worry, Richard," she said airily. "Melvin is wealthy in his own right. Far wealthier than me. You should see his home. It's magnificent."

"I'd like to. So how old, exactly, is Melvin, by the way?"

"Sixty-six."

Only one year older than his mother. A good match. Better than with his father, who'd been twelve years older.

"He sounds great. Better not keep him waiting, then. See you in the morning. Have fun," he called after her as she headed for the front door.

He wasn't sure if he heard right, but he was pretty sure she'd muttered, "I intend to."

The front door banged shut, leaving Richard to an empty house, but not an empty mind.

Sixty-six, he mused. Was a man past it at sixty-six?

He doubted it.

One thing he knew for sure. A man wasn't past it at thirty-eight.

Ignoring his growing sexual frustration was proving difficult. His male hormones, now directed where they normally went, had been giving him hassle. Yet there was no hope for them in sight.

It had been six weeks since Reece had put him in touch with the woman who ran Wives Wanted, a striking-looking but tough lady named Natalie Fairlane. Six weeks, and he wasn't any closer to finding a woman he wanted to continue dating, with a view to matrimony.

He returned to his laptop and brought up the photo of his fifth selection. Another brunette. She was as beautiful on the screen as the other four had been. But not one of them had had any effect on him in the flesh.

There'd been no chemistry, as Reece would have put it.

They'd all been far too eager to please him as well. He'd seen the lack of sincerity in their eyes. In a couple of them, he'd sensed downright greed. They'd chosen the most expensive food on the menu, *and* the most expensive wine.

That had been one of his little tests. Letting them choose the wine, of which he never drank much. No way did he want any decision he made influenced by being intoxicated. By the end of dinner, every one of the four had made it obvious they would be only too happy to accompany him home to bed.

Richard didn't think he was *that* irresistible to women.

He was a good-looking enough man. Tall and well built with strong, masculine features. His steely grey eyes, however, were on the hard side, he'd been told, and his manner was formidable.

Forbidding was the word one female employee had called him.

He supposed his approachability was not helped by his manner of dress, which could only be described as ultra conservative. The board at the bank preferred their CEO to look dignified, rather than sexy. The mainly pinstriped suits he wore *were* expensive, but not trendy. His dark brown hair was kept short. He shaved twice a day when necessary, and his after-shave was discreet. His only jewellery was a gold Rolex watch.

Women did not throw themselves at him as they did at Reece, or even at Mike, whose long-haired bad-boy image seemed to attract a certain type of lady. Probably the ones who liked to live dangerously.

No, Richard didn't think it was his natural sex appeal that had made his dates salivate by the end of each dinner. More likely the unlimited limit on his credit card.

So he'd sent each of them home in a taxi afterwards and returned home alone, where he'd filled in the questionnaire required after each date, ticking the box that said he didn't want to see the lady again and emailing it to Natalie Fairlane.

That was another of Wives Wanted's hard and fast rules. If either person didn't want to see the other again, that was it. *Finis.* If the female attempted further contact they were struck off the database. If it was the male doing the harassing, he was no longer a client of Wives Wanted.

No doubt this system was much better than going through a normal introduction agency or internet dating service. For one thing, the weirdos were weeded out. Richard knew he'd been put through an extensive background check before being accepted as a client. Ms Fairlane had informed him of this necessary procedure during his personal interview, at the same time assuring him that every girl on the database had been through the same security check, and was exactly what she purported to be.

Physically, at least, that was true. Each girl he'd dated had been as beautiful as they were in their photos.

But more and more Richard was beginning to think Mike was right. Most of these women were gold-diggers. Maybe Reece had just been damned lucky with Alanna.

But, having paid his money, he was determined to see the list through before giving up on the idea. He was planning to contact his fifth choice on the list when the front doorbell rang.

"Who on earth?" he muttered, standing up and making his way across the study and into the main hallway.

The Crawford family home was not a mansion, but it was spacious and solid, with the kind of character associated with houses built in Sydney's better suburbs in the nineteen thirties. Tall ceilings, decorative cornices, wide verandas, and wonderful stained-glass panels on either side of the front door.

As Richard strode towards the door the sunshine filtered through those panels, making coloured patterns on the polished wooden floor, then on the pale grey trousers he was wearing.

Wrenching the door open, the first thing he saw was a huge bunch of red roses. Followed by a face peeping around them.

A female face.

"Oh," the owner of the face exclaimed, her big brown eyes widening. "I wasn't expecting... I didn't realise..." She grimaced, then drew herself up straight, holding the roses at her waist, a bit like a nervous bride. "Sorry. I don't usually babble. Is Mrs Crawford home?"

"I'm afraid not," Richard replied, whilst thinking to himself that he already liked this girl much better than any on that damned database.

Yet she wasn't nearly as beautiful. Or as well groomed.

Her long dark brown hair was somewhat windblown. And there wasn't a scrap of make-up on her oval-shaped face. Her outfit of a wraparound floral skirt and simple blue T-shirt shouted department-store wear, not designer label.

But, for all that, he couldn't take his eyes off her.

"My mother's gone out for the day," he heard himself say whilst his hormone-sharpened gaze took in her ringless left hand.

Not that that meant much. She could still be living with someone, or be dating some commitment-phobic fool who hadn't snapped her up off the single shelf. That was one thing each of his Saturday night dates had bewailed over the dinner table. How many men these days didn't want to become husbands and fathers.

"She won't be back till very late tonight," he added. "Can I help you perhaps? I'm her son. Richard."

"Yes, I know that," she said, then looked flustered by her admission.

"In that case, you have the advantage on me," he replied smoothly. "Have we met before?" He knew damned well they hadn't. He would have remembered.

"No. Not really. I mean, I saw you at your wife's funeral. I...um...I did the flowers."

She seemed embarrassed at having to mention the occasion. On his part, Richard was pleased that he could be reminded of that day without too much pain.

Yes, he was definitely ready to move on.

"I see," he said as he wondered how old she might be. Late twenties perhaps?

"Please forgive me if I say I don't recall noticing the flowers that day," he said ruefully. "But I'm sure they were lovely. I presume these are for my mother?" he said, nodding towards the roses she was holding. Probably from crafty old Melvin.

"Yes. It's a phone order which was never picked up today. I know how much Mrs Crawford likes flowers—roses particularly—and I thought she might like them. I realise she's going away next Friday but they won't last that long."

"You know about Mum's trip?"

"Yes, she...um...told me about it herself last week. And about her new doctor friend. Melvin, isn't it? It's a pity, really. If she'd still been looking for a travelling companion, I might have applied for the job myself."

Richard was taken aback. "Why on earth would a girl like you want to travel anywhere with a woman old enough to be her grandmother?"

She shrugged. "Just to escape, I guess."

If she'd said to travel the world on the cheap, Richard might have understood. But to escape screamed something much more emotional. So did the bleakness that had suddenly filled her big brown eyes.

"Escape from what?" he probed gently. "Are you in some kind of trouble? Man trouble perhaps?"

She wasn't a raving beauty but, the more Richard looked at her, the more attractive he found her. She had lovely eyes, a sexy mouth and a fabulous figure.

He fancied her. Other men would, too.

She shook her head. "No, no, nothing like that. Here. Give these to your mother when she gets home, will you? Tell her they're from Holly. Just say they're a little thank-you present for all the times she's dropped in at the shop for a chat. She's a really sweet lady, your mum."

Richard refused to take the flowers. "Why don't you come inside and arrange them in a vase for her?" he suggested before she could cut and run. Any girl who wanted to get away that badly sounded like a girl who wasn't very happy with her life at the moment. If she did have a boyfriend, he sure as hell wasn't doing the right thing by her.

She blinked, then stared at him.

Richard had no idea what she was thinking, which in itself was as intriguing and attractive as she was. He'd been able to read those women he'd taken to dinner like an open book.

"Look," he said with what he hoped wasn't a "big bad wolf" smile. "I have absolutely no talent with flower arranging, whereas you'd have to be an expert. So what do you say, Holly? You do the flowers and I'll make us both some coffee. I'm good at coffee."

She still hesitated, making Richard wonder if he was easier to read than she was. Maybe she could see his intentions in his eyes. Not that they were evil intentions. He just wanted the opportunity to learn a bit more about her. He wasn't planning to seduce her.

Not yet, anyway.

"Who knows?" he said lightly. "Maybe Melvin will prove to be an utter bore and Mum will come home early, still looking for that travelling companion."

She laughed. "I don't think there's much chance of that happening, and you know it. You're just being nice, like your mum."

Nice. She thought he was being nice.

Richard's conscience stirred. But he swiftly put aside any qualms.

Faint heart never won fair lady.

"We will adjourn to the kitchen," he said before she had time to think up some excuse to flee. "This way." And taking her arm, he ushered her inside.

CHAPTER THREE

"I'LL JUST get you some scissors from Dad's study first," Richard said as he closed the door behind them.

When he abandoned Holly's elbow to walk up the hallway into a room on the right, a small shudder of relief rippled through her.

Having Richard Crawford answer the doorbell had been a real shock. She'd been expecting his mother.

But there he'd been, as large as life, and more handsome than ever, even more so than eighteen months earlier, when she'd first seen him. Gone were the dark rings under his eyes and that pale, haunted expression.

How wicked Holly had felt, finding him so attractive at his wife's funeral. The man had been in deep mourning, for pity's sake, shattered by the tragic death of the beautiful woman he'd married two years before. She knew from Mrs Crawford how much her son had adored his beautiful Joanna.

But all Holly had been able to think of whenever she'd snuck a peek at Richard Crawford that day was how impressive he looked in black. Her eyes had returned repeatedly to him during the service. She'd even envied his dead wife for at least having known the love of a man like that. Holly had been feeling extra lonely and vulnerable at the time, her father having passed away only a few months earlier.

For several weeks afterwards, she'd dreamt up all sorts of romantic scenarios where the handsome widower and herself would meet. But, strangely, not one had involved his being home, alone, when she delivered flowers to his mother's house. Neither did any scenario anticipate how intimidating she might actually find him in the flesh.

Intimidating. But still disturbingly sexy.

When he'd taken her arm just now, she'd felt almost paralysed by his touch, and his commanding physical presence.

Richard Crawford was a big man. Very tall and broad-shouldered, with large hands and firm fingers, and a manner to match.

She was grateful not to be in his presence at the moment. It gave her time to regather her composure.

But he'd be back any moment.

When he didn't return after a couple of excruciatingly long minutes, an agitated Holly tiptoed along the floral carpet runner till she could see into the room he'd entered.

His father's study, he'd said it was.

The room resembled more of an English gentleman's club than a study, with wood panelled walls, rich maroon velvet curtains and large leather armchairs. The desk Richard Crawford was rummaging through was a huge mahogany antique, which looked at odds with the very modern laptop sitting down one end.

Which was plugged in and on, she noted.

That explained the engaged signal when she'd telephoned. He'd been working. His mother said he'd become a workaholic.

But what was he doing here when Mrs Crawford was out? And why was he dressed the way he was, in smart grey trousers and a crisp blue business shirt? Add a tie and jacket, he'd be ready for the office.

Not many Australian men would be dressed as he was on a summer Saturday afternoon. Most would be lounging around in shorts and thongs.

Dave would have.

"Shouldn't be much longer," he said with a quick, upwards glance at her from under his darkly beetled brows. "I know they're here somewhere."

"That's all right," she replied. "Take your time."

He smiled at her. Not a wide, warm, infectious grin that had been Dave's trademark. A rather restrained smile.

Richard Crawford was different from Dave all round.

Of course, he came from a different world from Dave. A more cultured, educated world. And he was a lot older. In his late thirties at least.

Holly frowned at this last thought. Normally, she wouldn't look twice at any man his age. She was only twenty-six. All her boyfriends to date had always been around her own age, give or take a year.

Dave, the rat, had been exactly the same age.

Holly's thoughts turned bitter as they always did when she thought of Dave. Her only comfort was her recent realisation that she hadn't been truly in love with the creep. She'd just been fooled by his flattering ways. He was a charmer, was Dave.

A sales rep for a company that made cheap cards, he'd talked her into stocking his entire range within five minutes of walking into the shop. Talked himself into her life and her bed a week later.

Not that he was all that good in bed. But then, neither was she.

Dave had insisted she was, of course. He'd never stopped paying her compliments. Holly had come to the somewhat depressing conclusion since the demise of their relationship that he'd probably lied to her about everything, but especially that.

The man was a liar and a louse. Lots of men were these days.

But not this man, she thought as Richard Crawford looked up from the final desk drawer in triumph, a pair of scissors in his left hand. He was a man of honour. And depth. According to his mother, he hadn't even looked at another woman since his wife's death. What Holly wouldn't give to be loved the way he'd loved his wife.

"Thought I'd never find the darned things," he said as he rejoined her in the hallway. "The kitchen's down here," he added, then took her elbow again.

Holly shivered when another jolt of electricity shot up her arm, the same as the first time.

"It's cool inside these old houses, isn't it?" he said, thankfully misinterpreting her reaction as he ushered her down the hallway.

"Very," she agreed. But she didn't feel cool. Suddenly, she felt very warm indeed.

"Your mother didn't say you were staying with her," she began babbling again. "That's why I was so surprised when you answered the door."

"Just popped in to visit for the weekend," he explained, steering her into a large, homey kitchen with a dark slate floor and lots of pale wooden benchtops. ''Didn't know Mum would be going out. Mmm, I wonder where she keeps the vases?'' he said, stopping in the middle of the room to survey the U-shaped array of cupboards. ''You wouldn't happen to know, would you?''

Holly tried to will her heart to slow down. Useless exercise. It kept pounding away behind her ribs, regardless.

''Sorry,'' she said with a stiff little smile. ''I've delivered flowers here before, but I've never been inside. I'll just put these in the sink and help you look.''

''Good idea.''

She was still half filling the smaller of the two sinks with water when he said, ''Bingo! Vases galore down in here!''

Snapping off the tap, she turned to find him hunched down in front of one of the lower cupboards, the fine wool of his grey trousers stretched tight across his buttocks and thighs. His shirt was having a similar problem as it tried to house his broad shoulders and back.

Holly swallowed. This was crazy. She'd never been the sort of girl to ogle men's bodies. She'd never cared if her past boyfriends had muscles or not. She'd once filled in a survey in a women's magazine asking what it was that first attracted her to a man and she'd put eyes. Dave had had twinkly blue eyes to go with his winning smiles.

This memory had just entered her head when Richard Crawford's head turned and two wintry grey eyes lifted to hers.

A strangely erotic shiver ran deep inside her.

"Plenty of different sizes here," he said. "What do you prefer?"

It was testimony to her shocking state of mind that her thoughts immediately jumped to the size, not of the various vases on offer, but of the part of his anatomy that was thankfully hidden by his squatting position.

"I'll have that glass one there on the right," she said. How she didn't blush when he handed it to her, she had no idea.

Actually arranging the flowers was a blessing. She could concentrate on what she did best, and not even look at him as he busied himself making some truly mouth-watering coffee. Not the instant kind. The kind that percolated.

Unfortunately, he finished his job first, after which he settled on one of the kitchen stools to watch her work. She knew it was probably her over-heated imagination, but Holly could have sworn his eyes were more on her than the flowers.

"You really are good at that," he said.

"It's my job," she returned, pleased to hear her voice didn't betray her inner turmoil.

"Have you always worked with flowers?"

"All my life. My dad was a florist. He trained me."

"Was?"

"He died just over two years back. A stroke."

"I'm sorry. That must have been tough on you and your family."

"My mother's dead too," she told him. "She died when I was just a toddler. But Dad married again when I was sixteen. I have a stepmother and a stepsister, Katie, who's two years younger than I am."

Holly refrained from blurting out that both females were wicked witches, especially Katie. She didn't want to sound like a whinger. She'd cried out her sob story to his mother, though, when she'd come into the shop one day, soon after Dave had dumped her.

"How old are you?" he asked.

"What? Oh, I'm twenty-six."

"*That* young," he said in a way that indicated he had thought her older.

Holly's already battered self-esteem took this added blow quite badly. All of a sudden, tears welled up in her eyes. Thank God she wasn't facing his way, giving her the opportunity to blink them away and gather herself once more.

But the incident put a stop to her foolishly getting excited at being alone with Richard Crawford. Which she had been. No use pretending she hadn't. She'd been thinking all sorts of silly things in the back of her head, such as he'd been looking at her with admiration and asking her questions because he was attracted to her.

God, she was laughable. If and when Richard Crawford started dating again, it would be with a woman like his wife. A sophisticated stunner. Holly had seen a framed photo of Joanna Crawford at the funeral. Talk about gorgeous! She'd also been supersmart. A literary agent, working for an international publisher whose head office was in New York. Mrs Crawford senior had told Holly all about her daughter-in-law-to-be when she'd dropped into the shop to select a mother-of-the-groom corsage the day before the wedding.

What interest could Richard Crawford possibly have in a simple girl who arranged flowers for a living, was passably attractive at best and had never been further from Sydney than the Central Coast?

CHAPTER FOUR

RICHARD could not believe how much he was enjoying just sitting there in his mother's kitchen, watching this lovely girl put flowers in a vase.

And she *was* lovely.

He'd now had the opportunity to study her at length, noting the perfect shape of her profile, the lushness of her lips, the slenderness of her neck and arms. His eyes followed each graceful movement as she snipped the end of a rose, then lifted it into place in the tall vase.

Her figure continued to entrance him as well. Although only of average height, she was beautifully in proportion with the hourglass shape he preferred in a woman. Her breasts looked naturally full, with no artificial enhancement. Her bra was of the thin variety, her nipples clearly outlined against the soft blue material of the T-shirt.

He wondered momentarily if they were erect because she was cold, or because she was as sexually aware of him as he was of her. He had no way of knowing. She wasn't in any way flirtatious, which he liked. Joanna had been a terrible flirt.

But it would be good to have a sign that the attraction he felt was mutual. Were hard nipples a reliable sign?

''Are you still cold?'' he asked, and watched as she turned an annoyingly unreadable face his way.

"Cold?" she repeated blankly. "No. Not really."

Mmm. Maybe her nipples were always like that.

His flesh tightened at the thought.

"I don't think I should put any more of the roses in this vase," she announced, tipping her head charmingly to one side as she surveyed the arrangement of richly coloured blooms. "It's perfectly balanced right now. Any more would spoil it."

"You're right," he agreed. "It's perfect."

Just like you, he thought, and wondered how soon he could ask her out. Obviously, not till he found out her boyfriend situation.

The phone began to ring, which annoyed him no end. For one thing, it was out in the hallway and not in the kitchen.

"Won't be a moment," he said. "Why don't you find another smaller vase for the rest of the roses whilst I'm gone?" he suggested. He knew how awkward it could be, standing round at a loose end whilst people chatted on the phone. He didn't want her finding any excuse to leave.

It was his mother on the phone, being uncharacteristically but blessedly brief, allowing him to get back to Holly before she'd finished doing the second vase.

"That was Mum. I've been invited to go to lunch at Melvin's place tomorrow. Sorry, but I'd say the travelling companion job has definitely been taken," he finished, thinking of how eager his mother had been to get back to the new man in her life.

Holly gave him a wan little smile. "I never imagined anything else. Well, I'll be off, then, Mr Crawford. I don't think I'll stay for coffee, but thank you for the offer."

Richard was taken aback. Had he been overly optimistic, hoping the chemistry he'd been feeling was mutual? Maybe he'd lost the knack of knowing when a woman fancied him and when she didn't. Yet he'd been sure he'd sensed something in Holly's body language whenever their eyes had met.

Maybe she was nervous of him. He knew he sometimes made women nervous.

''You have something you have to go home for?'' he asked, and made eye contact with her again. This time he saw what he hoped he'd see. That flicker. That spark.

''There's always work to do when you run a business,'' she replied.

''Please don't go,'' he said with a smile that would have rivalled Reece's on the charm meter. ''I was really enjoying your company.''

She blinked. ''Really?''

''Really. And whilst we're having our coffee, I want you to tell me what it is you thought you needed to escape from?''

It took him a good half an hour to get all the details out of her—and to get her to call him Richard. But once the full picture of Holly's position was clear, he felt furious on her behalf. The poor girl. Betrayed by her boyfriend with her stepsister. Betrayed by her stepmother with the business.

And no one to stand up for her!

No wonder she wanted to escape. Why would she want to stay with a family who clearly didn't love her? Or continue to work hard for no rewards? Such a situation was not only unjust, it was untenable.

''You could have contested your father's will, you know,'' he pointed out sternly.

Her velvety eyes showed surprise. ''Really?''

''Yes, really. And it's not too late. If you like, I could put you in touch with a good solicitor.''

''No,'' she said, pulling a face and shaking her head. ''No, it's too late for that. Besides, Dad warned me never to take anyone to court. He said the only ones who got rich from suing people were the lawyers.''

Richard had to smile. That opinion was widely held by lots of people, but not true in the circles he moved in.

''That depends on the lawyer,'' he said, ''but it's your call.''

She sighed. ''If only Dad had changed his will and left me a controlling percentage of the business. I know that's what he intended to do. But, of course, he wasn't expecting to have a stroke at fifty-five, no more than my mother expected to be knocked down by a bus at twenty-five.''

''You seem to have had some rotten luck in life, Holly.''

''Things haven't been all that easy lately,'' she admitted.

''Why don't you tell your stepmother and stepsister to go to hell?''

''Trust me. I intend to one day. When the time is right. My plan is to stay on where I am till I've found a new job and a new place to live. That way I can go on living in the flat above the shop for nothing, and save some more money. I think I should keep my big mouth shut till I'm ready to move out, don't you?''

''No, I don't. I think you should tell them both exactly what you think of them right now,'' he ground out. ''Along with your bastard of an ex-boyfriend!''

How he would have liked the opportunity to tell Joanna what he thought of her! Instead, he'd had to grieve for her with all that bitterness building up within him. Bitterness and bewilderment. Her betrayal still ate away at him, whenever he thought about it. Why *had* she been unfaithful to him? He'd thought she loved him. She'd said she did. And acted as though she did.

But she couldn't have. Which meant she must have married him for his money. And the prestige of being Mrs Richard Crawford. She'd certainly loved their multimillion-dollar home at Palm Beach, and the wardrobe of designer clothes she'd constantly added to. Joanna had always claimed you could never wear the same dress twice when mixing with the high echelons of Sydney society. Not a weekend had gone by that they weren't going to some fancy dinner party, or gallery opening, or the races. Or all three.

Richard hadn't been enamoured with that life, but he would have done anything to make her happy. Love really did make a man blind. Women too, he supposed. Clearly, Holly hadn't been able to see her ex-boyfriend's true nature. Reading between the lines, it was obvious that this Dave had thought Holly owned the flower shop, and had dropped her when he'd discovered it was the stepmother—hence the stepsister—who'd inherited everything.

''That's all very well for you to say, Richard,'' Holly pointed out, an indignant colour creeping into her cheeks. ''You have a great job, according to your mother, and a great place to live, no doubt. You'd never have to live in a crummy bedsit, which is what I'd be relegated to if I shouted my mouth off prematurely. Connie would have me tossed out in the street."

Richard almost offered her free room and board at his penthouse right then and there. His room, preferably.

For a few perverse seconds, he indulged in the erotic fantasy of taking Holly back home with him tonight, of his taking off all her clothes and taking her to bed for the rest of the weekend.

But that was all it was. A fantasy.

He could see she wasn't the kind of girl who jumped into bed with men at the drop of a hat. Easy women, Richard realised, behaved very differently from Holly. They flirted, for starters. Fluttered their eyelashes and stroked male egos with constant verbal flattery. Joanna had been brilliant at that, always telling him what an incredible lover he was.

How many other men, he thought bitterly, had she said the same thing to?

Richard wondered if Holly was still in love with that bastard who'd dumped her for her stepsister. Love didn't die just because someone had done you wrong. Richard knew that for a fact.

Still, he was now convinced that romantic love was not the best foundation for choosing a wife. Besides being based on emotion, it was a poor judge of character.

Joanna's true character remained a mystery to him, whereas he already knew Holly to be sweet and soft, without a greedy bone in her body.

She was also wonderfully vulnerable right now. A quotation of Shakespeare's popped into his mind.

There is a tide in the affairs of men,
Which, taken at the flood, leads on to fortune;
Omitted, all the voyage of their life
Is bound in shallows and in miseries.
On such a full sea are we now afloat,
And we must take the current when it serves,
Or lose our ventures.

Richard decided then and there not to let the grass grow under his feet where Holly was concerned. It was clear he probably wasn't going to find a wife from Wives Wanted. Which meant he had to find one the old-fashioned way.

"You're right," he said. "There's nothing to be gained by shouting your mouth off. Far better to outwit your enemies. I do that at the bank all the time. So tell me, dear Holly, are you doing anything tonight? If you're not, how about letting me take you somewhere nice for dinner?"

CHAPTER FIVE

HOLLY just stared at Richard.

"I've shocked you," he said.

What an understatement!

She continued to stare at him, her head spinning.

"Is there any reason why you can't come to dinner with me?" he went on. "Have you found a new boyfriend since Dave?"

"Heavens, no!"

"Then what's the problem? You don't like my company, is that it?"

"No, no, that's not it at all!" she blurted out before gaining control of her tongue. "I um...I'm just surprised, that's all."

Floored was a better word. Why on earth would a man like Richard Crawford want to take a girl like her out to dinner? She wasn't a total dimwit where men were concerned, even if Katie said she was.

It came to her then that maybe Mrs Crawford might have been wrong about her son not looking at another woman since his wife died. It had been eighteen months, after all. Eighteen months was a long time for a man of Richard's age—of any age, for that matter—to go without a woman.

Could sex be the answer to the puzzle of his asking her out?

Holly knew she was a pretty enough girl, with nice eyes and the kind of figure men had always been attracted to. She had never had any trouble getting boyfriends. The trouble had always been keeping them.

Not that Richard Crawford would want to be her boyfriend. The idea was ludicrous! He might, however, be on the lookout for a one-night stand. A lot of men expected an after-dinner thank-you of sex these days.

Not that he would pressure her for it. Holly knew he wasn't that kind of man. But he was still a man, a man in his physical prime, a man with cold, sexy eyes and a great body and probably more sexual know-how than any man Holly had ever been with.

So why wasn't she jumping at the chance? Hadn't she fantasised about just this kind of scenario?

Actually, no, she hadn't. Her fantasies had been of his falling in love with her at first sight and wanting her till death did them part. Holly always gave her fantasies a happily-ever-after ending, not a "thank you for the sex but I don't want to see you any more" ending.

"What's worrying you?" Richard asked. "We're just talking dinner here."

"Are we?" she snapped before she could snatch the words back.

His eyes rounded slightly. Then he nodded. "Yes," he said. "We are."

Holly sighed. But was it with relief, or disappointment?

Still, she hesitated. Why, she wasn't sure. Maybe because she feared having a taste of something that she'd always secretly craved, but which had previously been well beyond her reach, even for a few short hours. How would she feel when the evening was over and she never saw or heard from Richard again?

At the same time, how would she feel if she said no and was left wondering what even having dinner with a man like Richard Crawford was like? He was sure to take her to a top restaurant in town, somewhere elegant and expensive.

Dave had been the king of the take-away meal. Even then, she'd paid for most of them. Holly knew she wouldn't have to pay for a single thing tonight. Except perhaps emotionally.

But the temptation was too great. ''All right,'' she said, a zing of adrenaline sending her heart into a gallop with her surrender.

''Wonderful,'' he said, and glanced at the gold watch on his wrist. ''It's half-past five. Shall I pick you up at, say…seven-thirty?''

''Seven-thirty will be fine,'' she said, doing her best to sound all cool and sophisticated, now that she'd accepted his invitation.

''How are you getting home?'' he asked. ''I didn't see a car outside when I opened the door.''

She didn't have a car. She had a van, which belonged to the business. ''It's just a short walk.''

''I'll walk you home,'' he offered.

''That's not necessary.'' She wanted to run home. She'd need every second of the time left to be ready. She'd have to wash her hair and blow-dry it, and do her nails and Lord knew what else.

''I'll walk you home,'' he repeated, his gaze as uncompromising as his voice.

My, but he could be masterful when he wanted to be. Holly wondered if he was just as masterful in bed. Not that she'd find out. Richard had said tonight was just dinner and he struck Holly as a man of his word. Darn it. Despite never having been a one-night-stand kind of girl, there were always exceptions to the rule, and, for Richard Crawford, Holly might have made an exception.

The Crawford house was on top of a hill, about half a kilometre from Strathfield railway station. Holly's shop was in a small block of three not far from the station, a reasonably good position for passing trade. There was a café, a hairdresser and her flower shop, right on the corner, all ancient brick buildings with awnings over the pavements and a second floor upstairs.

''Where does your stepmother live?'' Richard asked as they walked down the hill together.

''About a kilometre away,'' she replied. ''On the other side of the railway.''

''So how long have you lived in the flat over the shop?''

''I moved in not long after Dad died.''

''And why was that? Couldn't stand the wicked witches any longer?''

She smiled. That was what Sara had called them. ''Partly,'' she agreed. ''But I also felt closer to Dad there.''

''Understandable,'' Richard sympathised.

''I dare say Connie will sell Dad's house too, if and when the business sells. She's always wanted to live on the North Shore.''

''So how much would the business be worth?'' he asked.

''I'm not sure. I was too angry to ask Connie what

price she'd put on it. But over a million at least. It's a freehold property.''

''That's a lot of money to give up without a fight, Holly.''

''Yes, I know that. But it isn't the money so much as the business itself. Dad loved it. And I love it. I love working with flowers, you see. It makes me feel good. Flowers make people happy.''

''I still think you should take your stepmother to court. The shop should be yours. It's not fair.''

''Life's not always fair, Richard. Surely you must appreciate that,'' she added, then wished she hadn't. A sidewards glance saw that the muscles in his face and neck had tightened.

''You're right,'' he bit out. ''It isn't always fair, but you can't allow the injustices of life to beat you down. You have to fight back.''

''I *am* fighting back,'' she countered, stung that he might think her weak. ''In my own way.''

He smiled over at her. ''A quiet achiever,'' he said. ''Yes, I can see you are that, Holly. I apologise. I have no right to criticise. Or force my opinion down your throat. What's your second name, by the way?''

''Greenaway.''

''An apt name, for a florist.''

''You're not the first person to say that.''

''Sorry again. Is it a sore point?''

''No. Not really. But Dave used to tease me about it.''

''The dastardly Dave. God help me from ever being like him.''

''You're not. Don't worry.''

They walked on, Holly increasing the pace a little.

"I haven't walked down this road in years," Richard said as they finally reached the front of A Flower A Day, the large FOR SALE sign even more glaring from the outside. "I used to catch the train to and from high school so I came past here every day. I actually bought some flowers in here for Mum one year when I was about seventeen. Did your dad own it back then?"

"I'm not sure," Holly said as she retrieved the key from where she always hid it behind a drainpipe. "How long ago was that?"

"Twenty-one years."

"I think so. He bought it when he was about thirty. Look, I'd better get myself inside if you want me to be ready in time. I'm a female, you know."

"I did notice that," he said, and suddenly his grey eyes weren't cold at all. They travelled slowly over her body, telling her in no uncertain terms that he did find her attractive. *Very* attractive.

But as quickly as his gaze had heated up, it cooled, making her wonder if that imagination of hers had been playing tricks on her again.

"You'd better give me your phone number, in case I'm delayed for any reason," he went on. "I'm not dressed for dinner. I'll have to dash home and change."

Holly almost panicked at this point. Not dressed for dinner? He looked fine to her. What was he going to change into, a dinner suit? She didn't have a lot of seriously dressy clothes in her wardrobe. None, actually, now that she came to think of it.

"Where's home?" she asked as she pushed the shop door open, her mind busily searching her wardrobe for possibilities. If only she had one of those little black dresses, the kind that took a girl anywhere. But the only black outfit she owned was the suit she wore to funerals. Besides being very tailored, black was not her colour.

"East Balmain," he replied as he followed her inside the shop. "I bought a new apartment on the point there a few weeks ago."

"Oh, right," she said, not really listening to him. What on earth was she going to wear?

"I shouldn't be late," he went on, "but give me your number, just in case."

"What? Oh, yes, my phone number." She hurried over to the long table that served as a reception desk and work station, picking up one of the business cards from the stack that sat in a plastic stand on the corner.

"Jot down your cell-phone number on it as well," he said before she could hand it to him. "You must have a cell phone," he added when she lifted blank eyes to him.

"Yes, but..." She was about to say why would he want that when she wouldn't be seeing him again after tonight. But then she thought, why be so negative? He might be at a loose end another night and think of her. Who knew?

"Okay," she agreed, picking up a Biro off the table and writing the number on the back of the business card.

"See you at seven-thirty," he said after she handed him the card.

"Could you make it closer to eight?"

He nodded. "Eight it is, then." And he was gone.

Holly watched him stride past the shop window on

his way up the hill, watched him and tried to come to terms with the fact that in two short hours Richard Crawford would return to take her out. Richard Crawford. Mrs Crawford's son. The CEO of a bank. A man, not only of impeccable background and breeding, but impeccable dress sense.

"Oh, hell," she squawked, and dashed for the stairs.

CHAPTER SIX

BY FIVE to eight, Holly's nerves had reached lift-off.

She'd done the best she could with her appearance, but typically, when you were in a state, things went wrong from the start. She'd spent far too long trying to put together the semblance of a classy outfit, discarding everything in her wardrobe till finally she'd come across an outfit she'd bought for a wedding at least four years back, a three-piece number in pale blue.

It had a straight, calf-length skirt, a beaded camisole with a highish round neckline and a filmy over-jacket with three-quarter sleeves that shouted "wedding guest" at her when she put it on, but at least it didn't look cheap. If she'd had the time, she might have taken the hem up on the skirt, but an hour had skipped by before she could blink. It had been seven by the time she'd jumped into the shower.

Putting her hair up, as she'd mentally planned, had been out of the question. She always took ages to do it that way. So she'd blow-dried it dead straight, then hurriedly put the sides up with some clear combs.

By then it had been seven thirty-five, leaving only twenty-five minutes to do her make-up and nails. Not nearly enough time to do a good job. In the end, she'd settled for a fairly natural look with her face. Fortunately, she could get away without foundation, having clear skin that always tanned to a nice honey colour by the end of summer. A hint of blue eye shadow, a few strokes of black mascara, some coral lipstick and her face was done.

Her nails had presented a real problem, however. You needed steady hands to do your nails properly. Hers had been shaking like a leaf. After a couple of attempts Holly had given up, wiping the smudged coral polish off and leaving her nails totally au naturel. Fortunately, she always took care of her nails. She had to, with her job, so they were always neat and clean and well filed to a nice shape.

But she wasn't happy. She'd wanted to be perfect.

A swift glance at her bedside clock now showed two minutes to eight. She almost wished Richard would be late. She still had to put some perfume on, plus her earrings, if she could decide which ones looked best. The pearl drops, or the gold. She held a different one up against each ear but wasn't sure. Neither looked quite right, perhaps because the camisole was beaded.

The shop doorbell ringing made up her mind for her. Neither.

''Oh, God,'' she muttered as she shoved her feet into the ivory high heels that had been bought to go with the outfit, and which hadn't seen the light of day since. The same with the ivory evening bag. Sweeping it up from her bed, she headed for the stairs, totally forgetting the perfume till she reached the bottom. Too late, then. She could see Richard standing outside the shop window, not wearing a dinner suit, but looking sensational all the same in a superbly tailored black suit with one of those collarless shirts underneath. A steely grey, it was, the same colour as his eyes.

Taking a deep breath, she plastered a smile on her face and swept the door open.

Richard hadn't known quite what to expect. He knew girls of Holly's age tended to dress sexily these days, especially on a Saturday night. He'd seen them around town, wearing short tight skirts and even skimpier tops. Anticipating this, he'd teamed his new black suit with one of the trendier shirts Joanna had bought for him, and which he'd never worn. He hadn't wanted to look like an old fuddy-duddy next to his twenty-six-year-old date. It had been different when he'd taken the women out from Wives Wanted. They'd all been older.

When Holly emerged onto the pavement, dressed elegantly and very modestly, Richard breathed a sigh of relief. With that delicious body of hers nicely covered up, he wouldn't suffer too much physical torture this evening.

When he'd been showering earlier, his aroused body had regretted his earlier reassurance that he would keep his hands off. A lot of people went to bed on their first date these days, he tried telling himself. It wasn't frowned upon, nor seen as evidence of loose morals.

In truth, Richard liked it that Holly wasn't a flirt or a sexpot. As he watched her lock the door then turn to face him he decided he couldn't have his cake and eat it too.

"You look lovely," he said. "Blue suits you."

"Thank you. You do, too. I mean…you look very handsome."

Her blush was delightful, and perversely provocative. When the time came, he was going to thoroughly enjoy taking this innocent to bed.

And she *was* a relative innocent. Not a virgin, of course. He understood Holly had undoubtedly slept with Dave, and probably other boyfriends over the years. Girls who looked like Holly didn't stay virgins for long.

But she lacked the kind of sexual confidence that had oozed from Joanna. That was why Holly didn't flirt. Or dress to tease.

More and more Richard believed he'd found the right girl to marry. All he had to do now was make sure Holly would say yes, when he asked her. Which meant he had to make her fall in love with him. Or think she had.

The restaurant he'd chosen to take her to tonight was a good start, Richard reasoned as he opened the passenger door of his navy BMW. Nothing impressed women as much as an intimate dinner by candlelight in a five-star establishment. This place had certainly impressed the first of his dates from Wives Wanted.

High up in a building overlooking Circular Quay, Hal's Hideaway restaurant had everything. A magnificent view. A relaxing ambience. Discreet, but prompt service. A wonderfully diverse menu. And a cellar to die for.

"So where are you taking me?" she asked once they were on their way.

"To a restaurant in town, overlooking the harbour."

"What kind of food do they serve? I mean, is it Italian, or Chinese, or what?"

"The cuisine is international."

"Oh, dear, it sounds posh."

He smiled. "It is posh. But you don't have to worry. You look absolutely gorgeous."

"I look like I'm going to a wedding."

"Not at all. You look divine."

She laughed. "You know how to make a girl feel good, I'll say that for you, Richard."

He aimed to make her feel even better by the time the night was out. They chatted away amiably during the twenty-minute drive into the city, but by the time he'd parked the car in one of the spots especially reserved for Hal's clientele, then steered her up to the restaurant, she'd gone all quiet and stiff.

"I've never been to a place like this," Holly whispered after they'd been settled by the maître d' at one of the best tables in the house. Next to one of the wide windows that gave an uninterrupted view of the opera house and the bridge. "I won't have a clue what to order," she added with worry in her voice as she glanced at the menu, which was, admittedly, a bit daunting.

"Would you like me to order for you?" he offered. "I've been here before and I have a pretty good idea what the chef does best."

Her eyes showed relief. "Yes. Yes, I think that would be a very good idea. I'm not a fussy eater. I'm sure I'd like anything you like."

Let's hope so, Richard thought privately as his flesh stirred and his mind filled with the things he'd like to do to her.

"What about the wine list?" he went on. "Is there anything on it you especially prefer?" And he held it out to her.

When she took it, he noticed that she didn't have painted nails. Neither was she wearing jewellery, or perfume. Whilst this pleased him tonight—her lack of feminine artifice showed she didn't have any secret agenda where he was concerned—Richard was already looking forward to the nights when she would wear nothing else for him *but* perfume. She would look magnificent naked, he thought as his eyes surreptitiously raked over her. He could see her now, stretched out on top of his blue satin quilt, her dark hair spread over his pillows, her soft brown eyes slumberous from his lovemaking.

"I can't believe these prices," she said as she studied the wine list, a frown on her pretty forehead. "I do like wine, but I always buy it at a discount liquor shop. I've never paid more than twelve dollars for a bottle. I know they bump up the prices in these fancy restaurants, but there isn't a bottle here under seventy-five dollars. Most are over a hundred! Some of them are over two hundred!"

One of which his first date from Wives Wanted had chosen, Richard recalled.

"They're specialist wines," he told her, "from wineries all over the world. You won't find them on any shelf in liquor shops, especially discount ones."

She handed him back the list. "I'm sorry, Richard, but I wouldn't feel comfortable drinking wine at fifteen dollars a glass. That's outrageous. No wonder they didn't put any prices on the meal menu. I'll bet the food here costs a bomb as well."

Richard felt gratified that his character assessment of Holly had been correct. She was nothing like Joanna, or any of the women he'd dated from Wives Wanted. "Why don't you let me worry about the prices, and the choices? You just sit back and enjoy."

She opened her mouth, possibly to protest further, but then closed it again with a resigned shrug. "All right. I guess I can manage to ignore my suburban mentality for one evening. It will be something to tell my grandchildren about one day."

Richard smiled. He could live with that, provided they were his grandchildren as well.

The evening progressed nicely from that point. Holly seemed to relax—even if Richard didn't entirely. Difficult to be totally relaxed when he felt so aroused. But he discovered lots more to like about Holly during their four-course meal and almost two bottles of wine. She was remarkably well read, and even played bridge, which would make her popular with his mother. Apparently, her father had taught her and they had played together at a local bridge club. She also liked to keep fit and went to a gym three or four nights a week.

Richard thought of the many hours he'd spent in the private executive gym at the bank since he'd buried Joanna, working out his bitterness.

In future, he would work out for a different reason. To look good for this delightful girl. And to be extra fit. He wanted his body to be able to keep up with his mind.

And his mind had him making love to Holly for hours on end.

Midnight rolled around before he knew it. The

waiter offered them a complimentary cognac to follow their after-dinner coffee, but Richard declined. Although Holly had consumed more than half the wine, a cognac would surely tip him over the driving limit. So he ordered another coffee and they sat talking for another half an hour before he called for the bill.

"I think I'm a bit tipsy," Holly confessed when she stood up and swayed on her high heels.

"No worries," he said, and took her elbow. "You're with me."

"Yes…" Something like dismay flashed through her eyes. "Yes, I'm with you."

Richard thought about that moment during the drive home. Was she still pining for Dave? Wishing she'd been with him?

He resented that idea. A lot.

As much as he admired and desired Holly, there was no point in pressing on with a relationship if she was pining for some other man. If and when he married again, it would be to a girl who gave him her undivided attention and loyalty. This time, his wife would be the one madly in love with him, not the other way around.

"Thank you so much for tonight, Richard," she said rather primly as he angled his car into the kerb outside the flower shop. "Like I said earlier, it was an experience I will never forget."

Richard switched off the engine and turned to her. "Was it an experience you'd like to repeat?" he asked.

He could see her face quite clearly, his car parked underneath a corner street light.

Surprise zoomed into her eyes as she twisted in the seat to face him.

"You want to take me out to dinner again?"

"Dinner. Lunch. The theatre. The races. You name it, I'd like to take you there."

"Oh..." Her mouth fell open. And stayed open.

"But I only want to take you, Holly," Richard said as he reached over to place a gentle hand on her cheek.

Damn, but it was soft. *She* was soft. How he ached to bury himself in that softness, to feel her flesh close tightly around his, to lose himself in her.

"I don't want any third party coming along with us," he said, his eyes narrowing on her lush mouth. "No ghosts from the past. No wishing I was Dave."

"Dave!" she exclaimed. "I haven't given Dave a single thought all night."

"Good," he said, then abruptly closed the short distance between their mouths.

She sucked in sharply, but didn't pull back, letting his lips move over hers without protest. But without obvious pleasure as well.

His head lifted to find her staring at him with eyes like saucers.

"Don't you know how beautiful you are?" he said. "And how much I want you?"

She blinked and said nothing. She seemed frozen.

His hand stroked her cheek, then moved along her stiffly held jaw, drifting downwards to find the pulse that was throbbing wildly at the base of her throat.

Not frozen there, Richard realised, and kissed her again, this time slipping his tongue between her still-parted lips.

She came to life with a low moan, showing him with her own tongue that she liked that kind of kissing.

A raw triumph claimed Richard when she tipped her head back for him to kiss her even more deeply. He knew then that Dave was history.

It proved difficult to wrench his mouth away from hers. Clearly, she didn't want him to stop. On his part, his long-denied body was screaming at him to continue, to carry her inside the shop and ravage her on that work table.

But Richard wasn't going to risk ruining his long-term plans for any short-term pleasure. Holly was a woman. When sanity returned afterwards, she would remember that he'd promised to keep his hands off tonight. She might not be overly impressed.

He could wait one more week before satisfying his carnal urges. It wouldn't kill him.

Besides, he didn't really want a quickie. He wanted her in his bed at the penthouse for hours and hours.

"I'm sorry," he said swiftly. "I know I promised not to do that. I lost control for a moment," he added, which was almost true.

"It's all right," she said. "I…I didn't mind. Truly."

He stared hard at her. "Are you sure?"

She nodded, her eyes still dilated, her face flushed.

"Then you'll go out with me again?"

"Yes, of course," she said, her voice low and husky.

He touched her cheek again whilst he stared down at her mouth.

What wonderfully lush lips she had. He craved to have them all over him.

"I'd really like to take you somewhere tomorrow," he said, "but I have to go to Melvin's for the day. Then this coming week I'll be away, interstate, on business." Not a total lie. He did have to fly to Melbourne on the Monday for a few days. But he could easily have taken her out on the Thursday night. "Friday, I'm driving Mum and Melvin to the airport."

No. Richard wanted her to wait. Waiting would make her more susceptible to his desires, and her own. She might not be a woman of the world, but she was a healthy twenty-six-year-old girl who, till recently, had had a boyfriend. She was used to being made love to on a regular basis. It was obvious from the avid way she'd responded to his kiss that she was attracted to him.

"A friend of mine is having a party next Saturday night," he told her, his hand finally dropping away from her face. "You might have heard of him. Reece Diamond, the property developer?"

"No, no, I haven't," she said, confirming his earlier opinion that she'd led a rather insular life.

"It doesn't matter. You'll like him. Everyone does. And his wife, too. Her name is Alanna and she's a doll. Anyway, it's a house-warming party. Not of the casual kind, however. It'll be black tie. Reece doesn't know how to throw any other kind. He likes dressing up because he knows how good he looks in a tux. You'll need to wear something on the glamorous side if you don't want to feel under-dressed. Alanna usually goes for broke on these occasions."

Holly's eyes showed worry.

"If you don't have a suitable dress to wear," he said, "I'll buy you one."

"You certainly will not!" she said quite indignantly. "I can afford my own dress."

"Fine." Again, Richard was pleased. No fortune hunter here. Not like that piece he'd taken out on Friday night. He'd practically been able to see the dollar signs clicking away in her eyes.

"That's all settled, then," he said. "I'll walk you to the door." Which he did, resisting the temptation to kiss her again. Enough was enough. He wasn't a saint.

"I'll call you," he promised. "Tomorrow..."

And then he left her, without looking back. But he could feel her gaze on him all the way to the car. Once behind the wheel, he shot her one last glance through the passenger window.

She was still standing there at the door, looking forlorn.

Good, he thought, then gunned the engine. She wouldn't sleep much tonight.

There again, neither would he.

CHAPTER SEVEN

HOLLY was doing two hospital orders the following Monday morning, day-dreaming about Richard's call the previous night at the same time, when the bell on the shop door tinkled and his mother walked in.

Holly tried not to panic. Richard had warned her last night during his two-hour-long phone call that he'd told his mother about taking her out to dinner on Saturday night. Mrs Crawford had been surprised, apparently, but pleased.

The look on Mrs Crawford's face, however, was not the expression of a woman who was pleased. More like one who was perplexed.

''I came to thank you for the lovely flowers,'' she began with a puzzled frown wrinkling her high forehead. ''And to tell you how pleased I was to hear that Richard had taken you out somewhere nice on Saturday night. But I just noticed the FOR SALE sign on the window. Richard never mentioned that. Why are you selling, dear? Isn't the business going well?''

Holly heaved a great sigh of relief that this was what was bothering Richard's mother, *not* Holly's social or educational status. For a second there, she'd worried that Mrs Crawford thought a suburban florist wasn't good enough to date her precious son.

''It's not my idea, Mrs Crawford,'' she said. ''The business is actually doing quite well nowadays.''

''Don't tell me. I can guess. It's your stepmother.''

"Afraid so."

"But that's terrible. She has no right. I knew your father. He wanted *you* to have the business. You have to take that woman to court, Holly. Get what's rightfully yours."

Holly winced. Like mother, like son.

"I'd rather not, Mrs Crawford. Going to court is always so time-consuming. And nasty. And expensive."

"Richard has an excellent legal team at the bank. I'm sure he could help. I could ask him for you."

"He's already offered," she confessed, "and I refused."

Mrs Crawford rolled her eyes. "You're just like I used to be. Too soft. Life is cruel to soft women, Holly. You have to stand up and be counted. Act like a man, sometimes. I used to kowtow to Richard's father all the time. Frankly, I used to kowtow to everyone. But not any more. I don't intend spending the rest of my life turning the other cheek, or staying at home all the time. I've always wanted to travel, but I was too nervous to go alone. But I feel perfectly safe with Melvin. He's such a sweetie, and so knowledgeable about the world."

Holly didn't want to douse the woman's excitement by saying that she'd already had a detailed report about Melvin's good points from Richard last night, including his opinion that, the sooner the pair of them got married, the better.

"Sounds like Melvin might become more than just a travelling companion," Holly ventured.

A self-satisfied expression zoomed into Mrs Crawford's blue eyes. "Maybe. I'm not about to rush into anything. But you know, Holly, there's no better way to find out a couple's compatibility than to go away together somewhere. Being together twenty-four hours a day finds out the flaws in a relationship, I can tell you. I can still remember my honeymoon," she said, and actually shuddered. "If Melvin and I are still happy with each other after two months, then we might tie the knot. I have to confess that I have liked what I've seen so far. Melvin is a very good-looking man. And he has the most beautiful home. It's in one of Strathfield's best streets."

"Yes, but can he play bridge?" Holly asked, rather mischievously.

Mrs Crawford laughed. "You know me well, don't you, my dear? Yes, of course he can play bridge. It was the first thing I asked."

"In that case, you have my seal of approval. I..." The phone suddenly ringing made Holly forget what she was going to add.

"Would you excuse me a moment?" she said.

"A Flower A Day," she answered.

"Won't keep Richard at bay."

Holly immediately went hot all over. For a man who was on the conservative side in the flesh, he was quite the flirt on the phone. By the time he'd hung up last night she'd been as turned on as she'd been the previous night, tossing and turning in her bed into the small hours of the morning. And he hadn't even touched her. Just talked to her.

How would she react when he started making love to her? And he was going to. Next Saturday night. She just knew it.

"I'm sorry," she said, a shiver running down her

spine, ''but I have a customer and I can't talk right now. Could you possibly ring back a bit later?''

''Can't. I'm off to a board meeting and then off to the airport. Just wanted to ring and warn you before you went shopping for a new dress that Reece said there's going to be lots of dancing at the party.''

''What makes you so sure I'll be buying a new dress?'' she retorted in a teasing tone. She'd become a bit of a flirt on the phone as well.

''I'm thirty-eight years old, Holly. I know women. You wouldn't be seen dead next Saturday night in any old dress. Just don't buy a long one. I have a hankering to see you in something sexy and short, with a swishy skirt.''

''Swishy?'' she repeated, though her mind was still on sexy.

''Yes, swishy. Look, I won't keep you and I won't go bothering you with late-night phone calls for the rest of the week. I, for one, need some sleep before next weekend if we're going to be dancing the night away. See you next Saturday night, beautiful. At eight.''

''Don't you dare be late,'' she blurted out before he could hang up on her.

''I won't be,'' he returned with a dry laugh. ''Don't worry.''

Holly gripped the phone for a few seconds after he hung up, then slowly, and with a ragged sigh, placed the receiver back on its cradle.

When she turned back to Mrs Crawford, the woman was staring at her with a very thoughtful look on her face.

''That was Richard, wasn't it?'' she said.

"Yes," Holly admitted. "Why? What's wrong? Oh, I get it. You don't really approve of my going out with him, do you?"

"You're going out with him *again*?"

"He's taking me to a party next Saturday night."

"I see," the other woman said, then frowned some more.

"So can I. You don't think I'm good enough for him, do you?" Holly threw at her.

Mrs Crawford shook her head, her expression anguished. "It's not that, dear. Please don't think that. You're a lovely girl. It's just that you're not long over Dave and I…well…I wouldn't want you getting hurt again."

"You think Richard will hurt me?"

"I don't know what to think. All I know is that Richard has never gotten over his wife's death. It shattered him totally. You are the first girl he's taken out in any way, shape or form since Joanna's death."

"Forgive me for saying this, Mrs Crawford, but how do you know that? He doesn't live with you. He could be picking up a different woman every weekend and you'd be none the wiser. He's still a young man. You don't honestly think he's been celibate all this time, do you?"

Holly watched the cold, hard logic of her words sink in.

But the woman still shook her head. "I know my son. He has not been with any other woman since Joanna died and I can tell you why. He's still in love with her. He was crazy about her. You went to her funeral, Holly. You saw his grief. Don't go there, love. She spoilt him for any other woman."

''I don't believe that,'' Holly argued, thinking of the way Richard had kissed her. There'd been passion in that kiss and with passion came the possibility of love. Holly had been able to think of nothing else but Richard Crawford since the moment his lips had met hers.

''Your son genuinely likes me, Mrs Crawford, and I like him back. I fully intend going out with him next Saturday night and nothing you say will stop me.''

The older woman's blue eyes softened on her. ''I wouldn't dream of trying to stop you. You're one of the nicest girls I've ever met, Holly. Frankly, I like you much more than I ever liked Joanna. If by some miracle you and Richard find a future together, I would be the happiest mother in the world. But be careful. Promise me not to rush into anything. Will you promise me that?''

''Are you talking about sex?'' Holly retorted, flustered and angry by the woman's interference. The last thing she wanted to hear was how much Richard had loved his wife. Or that he was still in love with her. ''Are you asking me not to go to bed with your son?''

''No. No, I'm not asking you that. It might do Richard the world of good to go to bed with a girl like you.''

''What do you mean, a girl like me?''

''I mean a girl who's a giver instead of a taker.''

''His wife was a taker?''

Mrs Crawford shrugged. ''Joanna was...greedy. Greedy for life and greedy for Richard.''

But I'm greedy for him, too, Holly wanted to cry out.

She *had* to go out with him next Saturday night. Had to feel his lips on hers again. Had to let fate take her where it willed. Or wherever Richard willed.

''Maybe he's just lonely,'' Holly said in an attempt to defuse this conversation, which was in danger of getting out of hand. ''We all get lonely, Mrs Crawford. *I'm* lonely. It's not as though Richard and I are about to get married. We just enjoy each other's company.''

''You're right. I'm being melodramatic. I should be grateful to you for making Richard see that life is still to be lived. Please don't tell my son about this conversation, Holly. I won't, either. Promise?''

''I promise.''

''Forget what I said about his wife, too. He's awfully sensitive about Joanna. Clams up whenever I mention her.''

''I certainly won't be bringing his wife up,'' Holly said, unable to ignore the stab of jealousy over Richard still being obsessed with his wife.

But she could see that it was probably true. Probably true what *she'd* said as well. Richard was taking her out because he was lonely.

But that didn't make her own feelings any less intense. Holly couldn't recall ever losing this much sleep over Dave, not till *after* he'd dumped her. She couldn't recall any of Dave's kisses doing what Richard's kiss had done to her last Saturday night, either. She'd been mindless within seconds. Lord knew what would have happened if he'd pushed the matter further.

Instead, he'd stopped, leaving her more turned on than she'd ever been in her life. She hadn't wanted him to leave. She'd wanted him to stay and make love to her. Wanted him to bypass all those feelings of sexual inadequacy that had always plagued her.

"I...I have to get back to these flowers now, Mrs Crawford," she said, agitated by her thoughts. "I hope you have a wonderful trip."

"Thank you, dear. And take care."

"I will. I promise."

Famous last words.

A swishy skirt.

Well, it had that all right.

Holly stood back from the full-length mirror and twirled around once. The skirt flared out, but stopped short of showing her white satin G-string to the world. Which was just as well because the darned dress showed more of her body than any dress Holly had ever owned.

Made in pale pink chiffon, it was halter-necked in style, with a V-shaped cleavage slashed down past her breasts. Her already small waistline was cinched in tightly with a wide silver chain belt, making her full bust look even more voluptuous.

Of course, wearing a bra was out of the question. They didn't make frontless bras. Thankfully, the dress was fully lined, and draped in soft folds over her breasts, which minimised the visual impact of her naked nipples.

She'd bought the dress last night, at an expensive boutique in the city, driven to the extravagance by her desire to knock Richard dead when he picked her up tonight.

The salesgirl had raved, of course, saying it looked simply fab on her.

"Not many girls can carry this dress off," she'd said. "Most don't have the curves for it. Or the skin."

Holly knew what she meant. She did have smooth, honey-coloured skin with no freckles. To be honest, she'd thought she looked pretty fab in the dress, too.

But now that the moment was almost at hand—it was five to eight—her confidence was wavering. Had she gone too far with the dress and accessories, along with her hair and make-up? Would Richard like her dressed to thrill? He'd asked for sexy but maybe, once he saw her, he would prefer the more au naturel Holly of last Saturday night.

The phone ringing startled her. Oh, no, please, not Richard calling off our date, she prayed as she picked up the receiver with a shaky hand. She couldn't bear it.

"Yes?" she choked out.

"I'm outside," Richard said, "I can see a light upstairs, but the place is in darkness down here. Are you ready?"

"Ready as I'll ever be."

"No need to be nervous," he replied. "Reece and Alanna are very nice people."

"It's not them who make me nervous."

He laughed. "You don't have to be nervous of me. Now come downstairs this minute. I want to see what you look like."

The moment she came through that door out onto the pavement, Richard realised she *did* have to be nervous about him. Very nervous.

He'd expected her to doll herself up tonight. What he hadn't expected was to be totally blown away by the results. One glance at her in that provocative pink dress and Richard was consumed with a desire so hot and strong that his already-frustrated body was in danger of spontaneous combustion.

As he watched her lock the door he vowed then and there that she would not just stay the night with him. But all of Sunday as well. If he had his way, Holly would not be going home till Monday morning.

At last, she turned and walked towards where he was standing by the open passenger door, trying not to look too gobsmacked. Or too lustful.

''You look ravishing,'' he complimented, stepping forward to take her free right hand in both of his. Her left hand was swinging a cute little pink evening bag, which matched her dress. Her lips were pink, too. A slightly darker, brighter pink, the vibrant lipgloss making her mouth look wet and inviting.

A decidedly X-rated thought zoomed into Richard's mind. Not the first X-rated thought he'd had about her this week. He really was in a bad way.

He dropped his gaze swiftly downwards, lest the darkness of his desires showed in his eyes. Her high heels were silver, he noted, the same as that decadent-looking belt.

More appalling thoughts.

His eyes shot back upwards, past her braless breasts and that sinful-looking mouth.

Not much peace there, either.

Her hair was up in one of those sexy styles where loose strands fell around her face, covering half of her eyes and brushing sensually against her neck when she walked.

For a second he wondered if she was wearing panties, then decided that of course she was. Holly was not the kind of girl who would go without panties.

When he lifted her fingers to his lips she actually trembled.

"I'm going to be the envy of every man at the party tonight," he said as he straightened. "Shall we go?"

Holly did her best to pull herself together once she was in the car and they were on the way. But she could not seem to get her head around the way Richard had just looked at her. As if he wanted to eat her alive.

She hoped she hadn't looked at him quite so lasciviously.

But, dear heaven, black did become him.

She'd thought him handsome last Saturday night, dressed in that other black suit. In a black tuxedo, however, he looked not just handsome, but super-suave. Like James Bond on his way to an international casino.

Thank the Lord she'd gone to the trouble she had. And that he liked the way she looked. Nevertheless, Holly didn't believe Richard would be the envy of every man there tonight. She understood full well that this was going to be a party full of genuinely glamorous and beautiful women. It was being held at Reece Diamond's home, a waterside mansion in East Balmain not far from where Richard lived.

Richard had told her quite a bit about Reece

Diamond during his phone call last Sunday night, making Holly curious to see what kind of man he was. The most fascinating part had been how he'd met his wife, apparently through an introduction agency called Wives Wanted, a computer matchmaking service that catered for rich men who wanted beautiful wives, and beautiful women who wanted rich husbands.

Love was not precluded, but it was not high on the list of priorities with the clients of Wives Wanted.

Holly didn't like to criticise Richard's best friend, but privately she thought the whole deal sounded too much like legalised prostitution for her liking. She could not understand, either, why a man like Reece Diamond would need to employ such a service to find a wife. Richard had described him as charming and good-looking and highly successful. That didn't sound like the type of man to need help in finding a wife. It was a strange situation. But fascinating, in a way.

Holly was very curious to meet the wife as well. Alanna. What kind of woman put herself out there like that? If she was as lovely a person as Richard said, then why wouldn't she want to be loved?

Holly knew she could never marry a man she didn't love and who didn't love her.

Thinking of love and marriage reminded her of Mrs Crawford, and Melvin.

"Did your mother's plane leave on time last night?" Holly asked when they stopped at the first set of lights.

"Yes, thank goodness. I've never seen her so excited. Melvin, too. Truly, they were acting like giddy teenagers together."

"You really like Melvin, don't you?"

"Very much so. He's just what the doctor ordered for Mum, if you'll pardon the pun."

Holly laughed. Richard had a wonderfully dry sense of humour, rather like her dad.

"How did your business go this week?" she asked.

"It would have gone better," he replied ruefully, "if I'd been able to put my mind on it."

His head turned and their eyes met. Holly's heart stopped beating for a few seconds, before it lurched on.

"I...I know what you mean," she said huskily.

"I wonder if you do."

"I'm not a child, Richard."

His eyes dropped to her breasts, making her nipples tingle as they tightened.

"I can see that," he said.

"The...the lights have gone green," she told him shakily.

He said nothing in reply, just turned his eyes back onto the road and continued on, almost as though nothing had happened between them.

Lord, but she felt out of her depth with this man. His mother's warning popped back into her head, urging her to be careful. But she didn't want to be careful. She wanted to be reckless, and wicked. And she wanted *him* to be wicked.

She wanted his eyes back on her again. And his mouth. And his hands.

The wanting was acute and intense, a hunger that wasn't going to go away till it was satisfied.

Holly sucked in a deep breath, glancing at the clock on the dash as she slowly exhaled. Ten past eight. It wouldn't take all that long to get from Strathfield to East Balmain. Both were on the western side of the city. Balmain was a lot closer to the CBD than Strathfield, of course. A very trendy suburb these days. Very "in".

She needed to be there, to be surrounded by other people, to not feel the way she was suddenly feeling, as if she was in danger of losing total control of her life.

There she'd been last weekend, trying so hard to make sensible plans for the future, and along had come Richard Crawford, blowing them all out of the water. She couldn't think about a new job or a new place to live when all she could think about was him. She hadn't had her résumé done yet, let alone applied for any position. Instead, she'd gone out and blown nearly two thousand dollars on what she was wearing tonight.

Her perfume alone had cost over a hundred dollars, an exotic scent that was supposed to be irresistible to men. That was what it was called. *Irresistible.* She'd resisted the temptation to practically bathe in it, but she'd sprayed it in places she'd never sprayed perfume before.

Oh, God, some conversation was definitely called for.

"How many people know about Reece finding his wife through that introduction agency?" she blurted out.

"Only myself and Mike. So please don't spread that around. Reece told me in confidence."

Holly felt flattered now that he'd told her. He must really like her, and trust her, to tell her such sensitive information.

"I won't breathe a word. Who's Mike?"

"A computer genius friend of mine," Richard said. "And a very bad boy. So you keep right away from him, beautiful."

"I don't think there's any danger of my going off with some other man," she said rather ruefully. Didn't he realise how crazy she was about him? And how much she wanted him?

"You haven't met Mike."

"He must be a real charmer for you to be worried."

Richard laughed. "Mike has no charm whatsoever. Which for some weird and wonderful reason is his charm. I'm not sure what the attraction is for the ladies. He's not a pretty boy by any means. Looks like an escapee from the Russian Mafia. Always needs a haircut. Usually sports a five-day growth on his chin. But, for all that, there are some women—usually the oddest ones—who take one look at Mike and literally throw themselves at him. Maybe it's the challenge. Maybe they think they can change him. Little do they know, but he'll never change. Women are just rest and recreation to Mike. His life is his work, and making money."

"So why do *you* like him?"

"I guess it's because he's dead honest. And damn hard-working. You always know where you stand with Mike."

"Honesty *is* a good quality in a man," she admitted. ''And rare as hen's teeth. But, from the sounds of things, I don't think you need worry about my going off with this Mike.''

''Any man would be worried with you looking the way you look tonight,'' he said with a searing glance that set her skin breaking out into goose-bumps. ''That *has* to be a designer dress.''

''It's an Orsini,'' she confessed.

''Expensive?''

''Horribly.''

''You *should* let me pay for it,'' he said. ''You shouldn't be out of pocket, just because of me.''

''I told you before, Richard. I like to pay my own way.''

''I'll bet you let Dave buy you things.''

Laughter burst from her lips. ''You have to be joking. Dave never bought me a darned thing. No, I won't lie. He did buy me something once. A gold-plated pendant for my birthday last year. Must have cost him all of twenty dollars.''

''The more I hear about this Dave, the worse he sounds. Whatever did you see in him?''

Holly shrugged. ''Dave's a good salesman. As the saying goes, he could sell ice to Eskimos. He sold himself to me at a time when I was very lonely. My dad hadn't long died and I was beginning to see that my stepmother wasn't as fond of me as she'd pretended whilst he was alive. I'd always known Katie didn't like me, but I honestly thought Connie did. More fool me. I guess you could say I was ripe and ready to be conned.''

''We all get conned at one time in our lives.''

''I can't see *you* getting conned.''

''Can't you? Well, you don't know me very well yet, do you?''

The moment the words were out of his mouth Richard regretted them. Talk about stupid! He was supposed to be seducing her tonight, not putting seeds of worry into her head.

If tonight worked out as well as he hoped it would, he would soon be asking her to marry him.

One of the reasons he'd chosen this party to bring Holly to tonight was to show her the kind of life she could have as his wife. A life of luxury and security, of pampering and privilege. She would never have to worry about money. She could have anything she wanted, and so could her children. *Their* children.

His second goal tonight was to give Holly pleasure. Sexual pleasure.

Admittedly, he was keen to have some sexual pleasure himself. More than keen, actually. The situation was close to desperation level. Dancing with her was going to prove damned difficult. Just the thought of taking her into his arms and holding her close made his groin ache. Hell on earth, maybe he should have come to visit her on Thursday night. Then things might not have been so…hard.

Reece's address came into view, the street lined with parked cars. Reece did not throw small parties.

''We'll have to park down the road a bit,'' Richard said, driving slowly past the house, ''then walk back.''

He had to drive for quite a way, eventually finding a spot.

''Sorry about the walk,'' he said as he turned off the engine and retrieved his car keys. ''Will you manage in those shoes?''

He reached over to unsnap her seatbelt, bringing his face close to hers. Temptingly close. Before he could stop himself, his hand had lifted to encircle the soft skin at the base of her throat, sliding slowly upwards till it cupped her chin. Her eyes—what he could see of them—had definitely widened, her mouth falling open a little as well. Her perfume wafted up from that incredible cleavage, teasing him with its incredibly sexy scent.

One kiss, he thought. Surely one little kiss wouldn't hurt at this stage.

Her lips were ready for him. Ready and eager, flowering further open under his with a sound that was half sob, half moan. His tongue had slipped past them before his brain could stop it.

The rest of his body wasn't obeying him, either.

The desire for more than one little kiss kicked in with a vengeance and he found himself pressing her head back against the car seat, keeping her firmly captive there with his mouth whilst the hand that had been holding her chin slid down into the deep V of her neckline, finding its way like a homing beacon under the soft pink material and over one exquisitely naked breast.

Her back arched away from the seat, her mouth gasping under his. His tongue withdrew, his head lifting to watch her eyes dilate whilst he moved his palm back and forth across her already hardened nipple.

She seemed to have ceased breathing, her eyes round, their pupils hugely dark.

"Oh, please," she choked out when his hand stilled.

Her abject plea evoked a dark sense of triumph.

Later, he promised himself as he removed his hand. Later, he would make her beg again. But next time, she would be totally naked. And there would be no stopping. Not till she was crying out with one release after another. Not till she was entirely, totally his.

CHAPTER EIGHT

HOLLY closed the door of the ladies' powder room behind her.

What ordinary house, she thought agitatedly as she washed her hands, had two guest powder rooms, one for the gentlemen and one for the ladies?

But of course this wasn't an ordinary house. And these weren't ordinary people. The rich and the famous abounded out there. The wheelers and dealers of this world. Aside from her ultraglamorous host and hostess, Holly had already been introduced to two top politicians, a well-known television anchor-man and a famous actor with his new third wife, a gorgeous young thing twenty years his junior.

Holly felt she'd held her own, despite the company and despite being totally rattled by what had happened out in the car less than fifteen minutes earlier. But as soon as she'd been able to, she'd excused herself and asked directions to the powder room.

Now here she was, alone for a few precious moments, desperately trying to stop herself from thinking she'd fallen wildly in love with Richard Crawford.

Okay, so he was a good kisser. Lots of men were good kissers. Dave had been a pretty good kisser.

But once again, Holly could not remember responding to any of Dave's kisses the way she responded to Richard's kisses—with such utter abandonment of her own will. She would have let him do anything to her. Right there in his car. In a public street, for pity's sake.

She cringed when she recalled how she'd practically begged him to keep caressing her breast, which was still throbbing inside her dress. *Both* breasts were throbbing, even the one he hadn't touched.

What bewildered her the most was how cool Richard had been about it all. Cool and composed. Yet he was the man, wasn't he? Weren't men supposed to be turned on more easily than women? Weren't they the ones who usually lost control first?

Dave had been very impatient at times to get her into bed. Holly had quite enjoyed his lovemaking—when she wasn't worried about her own performance—but had never even come *close* to desperation, let alone begging.

Her face flamed with the memory. Was that why she wanted to believe she was in love with Richard? Would she feel better—less slutty—if it was love making her act so…so…

The door of the powder room opened and in walked her hostess, Alanna Diamond.

Richard hadn't exaggerated when he'd said Mrs Diamond was lovely. She was. A natural blonde, if Holly was any guess, her fine creamy blonde hair was styled into soft waves that framed a face that almost defied description. An angel's face. Delicate features. Huge green eyes. A soft mouth. And skin that was as fair and silky smooth as the rest of her.

Her dress was not the dress of an angel, however. Made in champagne-coloured satin, it was long and slinky, with spaghetti straps and a neckline that might have looked tacky if she hadn't had small, firm breasts. Her nipples were prominent, however. Round and hard. Like pebbles.

Age-wise, she was possibly around thirty. From a distance she looked younger, but up close Holly could see life's experience in and around her eyes.

"Hi there," Alanna said. "I'm so glad I caught you in here by yourself. I wanted to speak to you about something and I couldn't in front of the others. Reece would have killed me. Richard, too, I imagine."

"Oh?" Holly was at a loss.

"Reece told me a few weeks back that he'd put Richard in contact with the Wives Wanted agency and…well…you see, you might not know this, but I was one of Natalie's girls too, and… Oh, dear! I can see by the look on your face that you're embarrassed that I've brought this up. You're right. I shouldn't have. I'm sorry."

Holly wasn't embarrassed so much as stunned. *Richard* had been seeking the services of Wives Wanted? *Her* Richard, the one who'd just been making love to her in the car? The same Richard whose mother had proclaimed had never even *looked* at another woman since his wife died?

Holly couldn't think straight for a moment. If Richard was on the lookout for a wife of convenience, then what was *she*? A potential candidate, or a sexual stopgap to tide him over till he found the right woman to marry?

She opened her mouth to indignantly deny that she was one of Natalie's girls, whoever Natalie was. But at the last second, Holly bit her tongue. Whatever

Richard's agenda was where she was concerned, *he* obviously wasn't going to tell her the truth.

His mother sure didn't know her precious son as well as she thought she did.

Holly had to find out what was going on here.

"Please don't apologise," she said. "The thing is, I'm not…um…one of Natalie's girls. I do know about the Wives Wanted agency, though," she added swiftly. "Richard told me about it the other day. And, yes, he did mention that was how you and your husband got together."

"Oh, dear, now I feel even worse. I wish Richard had told Reece all this. But you know men. They just don't communicate the way we women do," she added with an exasperated shrug of her slender shoulders. "So how *did* you and Richard meet?"

"I was delivering some flowers to his mother's house last weekend. Hc happened to be home on a visit. Mrs Crawford was out and Richard answered the door. I'm the local florist."

"Oh, how romantic! There again, Reece says Richard's always been a romantic. He wasn't at all convinced that Wives Wanted was the right way for Richard to find a wife, but Richard was adamant at the time. Of course, after what happened to Joanna, you could understand why he might not want to fall madly in love again. Oh, Lord, there I go again! You do know his first wife was killed in a car accident, don't you?"

"Yes. I did the flowers at her funeral, actually. I've known Richard's mother for years. I just didn't meet Richard himself till the other day."

"Phew! Thank God I didn't put my foot in my

mouth twice in five minutes. So tell me, what do you think of Richard? I can see he's very taken with you.''

''We've only been out once together before tonight,'' Holly said. ''For dinner last Saturday night. But what I know, I like. Still, I would never consider marrying any man I didn't love. Or who wasn't madly in love with me.''

''Yes, well, we women all think that at some time in our lives,'' Alanna remarked ruefully. ''Sometimes it's better to settle for something less...intense. Something less dangerous.''

Holly blinked. ''Dangerous? What do you mean by dangerous?''

''Men who are madly in love can become very jealous, and irrational. Even violent. I prefer a less volatile relationship, especially in a marriage. Reece and I have a wonderful understanding of each other's needs. He gives me what I want and I give him what he wants. We're a darned good team, even if I say so myself.''

She looked Holly up and down with thoughtful eyes. ''You're a very attractive girl, but a few years younger than most of the women at Wives Wanted. When you get older, you might think differently. But if you want my advice, you could do a lot worse than to marry Richard. He's a good man.''

''He hasn't asked me to marry him. I'm not sure he ever will.''

''Oh, I think he will.''

Holly didn't know whether to feel flattered, or furious.

''If he does, then I'll be saying no,'' she said firmly, and told herself she meant it. ''Especially if

he Harlequin Reader Service® — Here's how it works:

cepting your 2 free books and mystery gift places you under no obligation to buy anything. You may keep the books d gift and return the shipping statement marked "cancel." If you do not cancel, about a month later we'll send you 6 ditional books and bill you just $3.80 each in the U.S., or $4.47 each in Canada, plus 25¢ shipping & handling per book d applicable taxes if any.* That's the complete price and — compared to cover prices of $4.50 each in the U.S. and 25 each in Canada — it's quite a bargain! You may cancel at any time, but if you choose to continue, every month we'll nd you 6 more books, which you may either purchase at the discount price or return to us and cancel your subscription.

erms and prices subject to change without notice. Sales tax applicable in N.Y. Canadian residents will be charged plicable provincial taxes and GST. Credit or Debit balances in a customer's account(s) may be offset by any other tstanding balance owed by or to the customer.

If offer card is missing write to: Harlequin Reader Service, 3010 Walden Ave., P.O. Box 1867, Buffalo NY 14240-1867

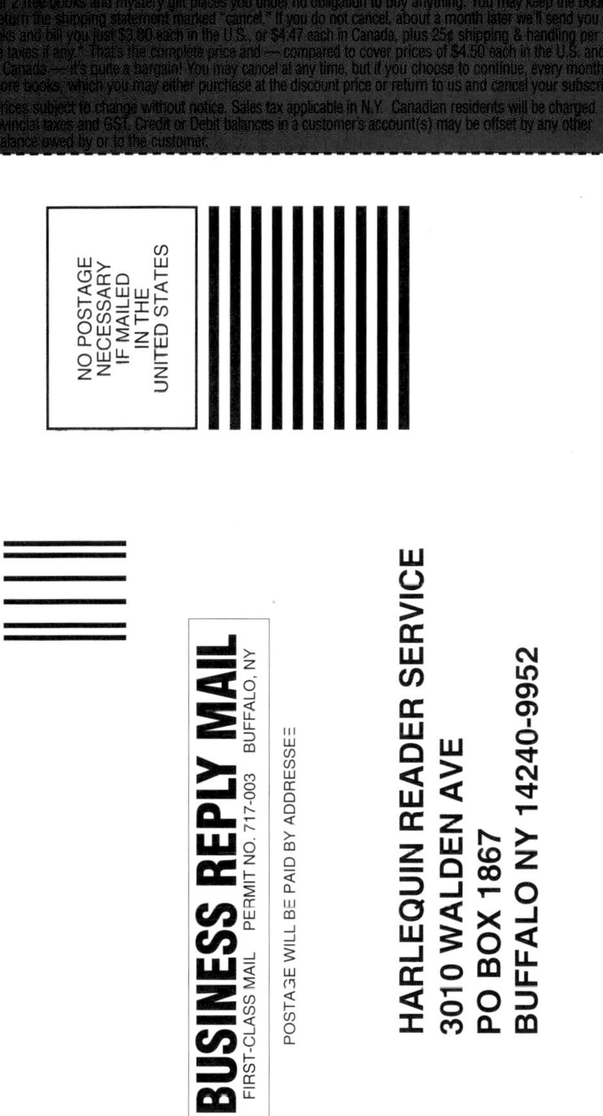

he's still in love with his wife. Which his mother warned me is the case.''

''Does that bother you?''

''Yes, it does.''

''In that case, definitely don't marry him,'' Alanna said with a hint of coldness in her voice. ''Jealousy is a curse. Now, I must get back to my guests. I'll just make sure I'm still decent first.''

When she turned around to check the back of her dress in the long mirror hanging on the powder-room door, Holly's eyes widened. She'd thought her own dress was borderline in modesty but the back of Alanna's dress—which she hadn't seen earlier—left absolutely nothing to the imagination.

Mainly because there *was* no back. The only thing stopping the entire creation from sliding off her slender curves were the spaghetti straps that crossed at her shoulder blades and attached at the sides just above her waist.

What had Holly really staring, however, was how low the dress was cut at the back, plus the way it clung to Alanna's well-toned buttocks. No way could she be wearing any underwear at all!

''Reece likes me to dress sexily, but I think he's gone a bit too far this time,'' Alanna remarked as she tried to hitch the dress higher, all to no avail. ''I'm going to start choosing my own evening gowns in future. Are you finished in here, Holly? If so, we can go back together. But not a word about this conversation to the men.''

''Absolutely not,'' Holly agreed.

But Alanna had given her plenty to think about.

She still wasn't convinced Richard ever intended

asking her to marry him. It seemed more likely he just wanted some sex from her. Surely, he would marry someone more like his wife. Someone older and more sophisticated and better educated. Someone from this Wives Wanted agency.

And if you're wrong, Holly? What if he *is* targeting you as the next Mrs Richard Crawford?

A tiny shiver rippled down her spine by this thought. So much for her declaration that she wouldn't marry a man who wasn't madly in love with her!

Still, Alanna's marriage to Reece seemed to be successful, she reasoned. Maybe a loveless marriage *could* work. Provided the sex side of things was all right.

No doubt Alanna didn't mind sleeping with her very handsome husband.

But for how long? Yes, how long before Alanna began to feel as if she was just being used, till she realised that her role in her husband's life was little more than that of a trophy wife?

Was that what Richard wanted of her?

Holly wished she felt more repulsed by the idea of being Richard's trophy wife. She'd talked holier than thou to Alanna, but would she really say no to marriage, if he ever asked her?

Holly was quite grateful to return to the party with her hostess by her side. With all these thoughts tumbling through her head, she needed someone with her as a buffer. She didn't want to say anything to Richard to spoil their night together and she was afraid she might do that. Her temper was already simmering at his not being open and honest with her.

Logic came to her rescue before her resentment could boil over. Why *would* Richard have told her about his being a client of Wives Wanted? A man of his personality and pride would keep such a thing a secret.

But what on earth *was* the attraction of a match-making service with these two men? They could have their pick of women. Surely.

Holly could only conclude that neither of them wanted love, or romance. They just wanted a beautiful woman to share their lives, and their beds. Not such a terrible crime, she supposed. But rather cold-blooded.

She shivered again.

Holly and Alanna found Richard and Reece standing out on the magnificent back terrace, which overlooked a resort-style pool and the water far below. The two friends were deep in conversation as they approached, giving Holly the opportunity to study both men. To compare them physically.

Reece Diamond was a flashy-looking individual, handsome in a decidedly Hollywood style, with bedroom blue eyes and streaky blonde hair that flopped sexily across his forehead. In a way, he had everything. The face. The body. The outgoing personality. He was drop-dead gorgeous to look at. Eye candy of the highest order.

But for all that, Holly infinitely preferred Richard's looks, with his dark hair, deeply set grey eyes and strongly masculine features. Maybe he wasn't quite movie-star material, but he was extremely attractive and very well built. He also had subtle layers to his persona whereas Reece was all out there, with everything he was and everything he owned on show.

Which included his trophy wife.

Alanna said she gave her husband everything he wanted.

Holly only had to look into that man's eyes as his wife walked towards him to see what it was Reece wanted from her. Holly imagined Alanna would be "on call" every single night.

Holly's insides tightened at the thought of being "on call" for Richard on a daily basis.

"Mike's just rung," Reece said straight away to his wife. "He's not coming. He sends his apologies."

"That's a shame," Alanna replied as she slid her hand through the crook of her handsome husband's arm. "I was looking forward to giving his latest girlfriend the once-over. You said she was a stripper, didn't you, darling?"

"Yes. That poor boy has no taste in women," Reece purred, bending to press his lips against his wife's bare shoulder. "Not like us, Richard. But I dare say he'll be happy enough with her, for the short time she'll last."

"I don't like men who treat women as sex objects," Holly said before she could think better of it.

"Some women don't seem to mind," Reece returned silkily, extracting his arm from Alanna's, then snaking it snugly around her waist, his hand coming to rest just under her right breast.

Holly found herself staring at it and wanting, not Reece's hand on her, but Richard's. And not *under* her breast, but right on it.

Her eyes lifted to Richard's, only to find them fixed on her cleavage.

Maybe he'd been wanting exactly the same thing.

When their eyes finally connected, Holly swallowed. Richard was looking at her exactly the same way Reece Diamond had been looking at his wife. With naked desire, not tenderness or affection.

Yet her heart flipped over just the same.

"I'd like to show Holly around the grounds," Richard said suddenly, his eyes not leaving hers. "The view is wonderful from the jetty."

"Why not take a bottle of champers and a couple of glasses with you?" Reece suggested. "If you wait a sec, I'll dash in and get them for you." And he did just that, returning in no time to hand everything to Richard, whispering something to him at the same time.

"What did Reece say to you just now?" Holly asked tautly before they'd even made it down the first flight of flagstone steps.

"He told me where he hides the key to the boathouse."

A boathouse. A much more private spot than a jetty.

"I don't want to go into the boathouse," she said rather sharply. She didn't trust herself to be that alone with him right now. Or vice versa.

"That's fine," he returned affably enough. "What do you want to do, then?"

"Can't we just walk? And talk?"

"Absolutely," he said, and they moved off again, making their way slowly down more flagstones.

"I would never want the kind of marriage Reece

and Alanna have,'' Holly said, and waited nervously for Richard's reaction.

''What's wrong with their marriage? They're very happy.''

''Maybe, but how long can it last, especially without children?''

''What makes you think they won't have children?''

''Oh, come on, Richard, just look at the way Reece dresses his wife.''

''What do you mean?''

''Alanna told me he chooses a lot of her clothes. If tonight's dress is any guide, he doesn't give a damn how much of her is on display. It probably turns him on to make other men jealous of him. She's like a married mistress, not a real wife. He won't want to risk spoiling her figure with a baby.''

''You're entitled to your opinion, but you're wrong. Reece was saying to me the other day they were going to try for a baby soon. As far as Alanna's dress is concerned, lots of women wear sexy evening clothes nowadays.''

''But she didn't have any underwear on!''

''Now that's the pot calling the kettle black, don't you think, beautiful?''

She hated the colour that zoomed into her cheeks. ''I'm wearing panties. And my top is lined. Unlike you-know-who.''

He laughed. ''You-know-who is an adult woman who went into her marriage with her eyes well and truly open. Look, I suggest you stop getting yourself so het up over Reece and Alanna's marriage. It has nothing to do with us.''

Richard was right. She *had* been getting all het up about Alanna's marriage. Perhaps because she was afraid Richard would talk her into a similar marriage. Afraid that she might like the idea of being his married mistress.

She could see him now, taking her into the kind of boutique that sold sexy dresses and outrageously erotic lingerie. She would have to parade everything for him. In her mind's eye she could see herself in a black satin corselette with suspenders and black stockings and shockingly high heels. And no panties, of course.

He would command her never to wear panties once she was his wife. She was to be always accessible to him, even when she visited him at the bank. She would be in a permanent state of arousal, always ready for him.

Always…

Holly sucked in deeply, then let out a long, slow, shuddering breath.

This has to stop, she told herself, but remained shaken by her fantasies.

''That view is pretty spectacular,'' she said as her eyes lifted to focus on the bridge, and the city beyond.

Richard laughed. ''What an understatement. That view cost Reece ten million dollars.''

''My God,'' she exclaimed. ''He must be very rich.''

''He is,'' Richard said. ''At the moment. His fortune tends to fluctuate. A few years back, he was practically bankrupt.''

''What happened to turn things around?''

''Two things. There was this savvy banker who

backed him when he wanted to borrow more money to buy land and houses. Then there was the property boom.''

''Aah. So that's how you two became friends.''

''Yes. I lent him some of my own money as well. Not just the bank's. Same with Mike, when he wanted to start up his software company. Both were very rewarding investments.''

''So you're as rich as Reece?''

''Actually, no,'' he said, then added as cool as you please, ''I'm a lot richer.''

CHAPTER NINE

FOR the second time tonight, Richard regretted his words, plus his moment of vanity.

The look Holly gave him was not the same kind of look his dates from Wives Wanted would have responded with, if he'd outlined his wealth to them.

Not that Richard could read exactly what Holly was thinking. The only time he could do that for certain was just after he'd been kissing her. He knew what she was thinking at those moments.

Nothing at all.

Right now, however, her far-too-intelligent brain was ticking over. Richard suspected his character was being assessed, and possibly found wanting.

''Of course, money isn't everything,'' he went on, going into damage control. ''But it can make life a little easier.''

She laughed. ''Oh, I'm sure it can. But I would imagine it could be very corrupting, to be able to buy whatever you want.''

Richard wondered where this edge had come from that he was suddenly hearing in her voice. It occurred to him that he should never have told her the truth about Reece's marriage. Holly was far too young and inexperienced to understand where a man like Reece was coming from. She certainly would never appreciate what had made *him* the man he was today. Holly might have been hurt by that Dave bloke, but she hadn't been devastated.

Bringing her here tonight was a mistake. He'd been hoping to impress her. Instead, he might have ended up alienating her.

The thought that the night would not end the way he wanted it to end had Richard's hands closing tightly around the bottle of champagne and the two crystal flutes he was holding.

"Do you want to leave?" he asked abruptly.

"Leave?" Her eyes flared wide. "Why would I want to leave?"

"You don't seem happy here. You obviously don't like Reece and Alanna, or this kind of party."

"But I do! I mean…I think Reece is a bit much, but I do like Alanna. Truly, I do. I think their house is fabulous. This party, too."

"Then what is it? What's wrong? Is it me? Are you angry with me for some reason? Are you upset over what happened out in the car?"

This was her chance to tell him, to bring the issue out into the open. But if she told him she knew about his connection with Wives Wanted, she would be breaking the promise she'd made to Alanna.

Holly did not break promises.

"No," she said. "No, I'm not upset over that. I guess I just feel a little out of my league here, Richard. Everyone is so sophisticated and I'm…" She broke off with a shrug.

"You are not out of your league," Richard insisted. "You are beautiful and intelligent and as good as any person here."

She stiffened. "Don't flatter me, Richard. I had enough false flattery from Dave to last me a lifetime."

"I'm not flattering you. I mean every single word. You're a very special girl, Holly."

She stared into his eyes, trying to see what he saw when he looked at her. Was he sizing her up as a potential wife, or buttering her up for his bed later tonight?

Thinking about actually going to bed with Richard after this party was over brought Holly up with a jolt. Oh, Lord, now that was where she would be *way* out of her league!

Yet she knew that was what Richard wanted. What she wanted, too. She'd thought about little else all week.

But if he was expecting an accomplished lover, then he was in for a shock. She supposed she wasn't utterly hopeless in bed. But she did feel a failure, the way she couldn't seem to lose herself in sex like some people seemed to. There'd never been any bells ringing for Holly, or stars exploding in her head, or whatever happened when you had an orgasm.

Still, maybe things would be different with Richard. It had certainly been different each time he'd kissed her. Very different when he'd touched her bare breast earlier on.

A shudder of remembered pleasure ricocheted through her.

"It's a little fresh out here," she said. "Perhaps we should go back inside. I can hear dancing music."

"Do you like dancing?" Richard asked as they turned and headed back up to the house.

"Yes, I do. What about you?"

"I'm no Fred Astaire but I can hold my own."

"I'll bet you can. I'll bet you're good at everything."

He laughed. "Now who's using flattery?"

"But you are good at everything, aren't you?"

Their eyes met, and his were extremely confident. "I always do my best."

Richard didn't drive her home after the party. He drove straight to his nearby apartment block, using his key-card to gain entrance to the private car park in the basement. He slid the BMW into one of his three allotted parking bays, turned off the engine and withdrew his car keys before glancing over at Holly, who hadn't said a single word since Reece and Alanna had waved them off.

He understood why. The time for small talk was over.

Any momentary worry earlier on that the evening would not end as he'd hoped had long disappeared. She hadn't been able to hide her own desire when they'd danced together. She'd pressed herself against him, her body language much more telling than her eyes ever were.

"We'll be more comfortable here than your place," he told her, his own tension on the rise.

Her head turned slowly towards him. If she was shocked by his presumption, she didn't show it. She did, however, seem somewhat dazed, or drugged, like someone about to go in for a major operation. Possibly she was a little drunk. She'd consumed the majority of that bottle of champagne over the evening. He'd restricted his intake, since he was driving. Still, he'd made sure she ate as well, not wanting her plagued by feeling sick tonight, or having a hangover in the morning.

"Stay where you are," he commanded. "I'll come round and help you out."

"All right," she replied, then sighed a deep sigh.

Richard frowned as he hurried around to the passenger door. He hoped she wasn't exhausted. They'd danced quite a bit. When he yanked open the car door and bent to release her seat-belt, their eyes connected.

"Don't kiss me down here," she warned him huskily.

Richard smothered a sigh of relief. She wasn't drunk. Or exhausted. Just turned on.

He knew exactly how she felt.

Straightening, he took her nearest hand and helped her out, slamming the door behind them and zapping the car locked.

"My…my purse," she said shakily when he started guiding her towards the lift well. "It's on the back seat."

"Leave it."

"But…"

"Leave it, Holly."

Holly left it, her mouth drying appreciably as Richard led her over to a lift door, which quickly opened when he pressed the up button. As he ushered her inside she felt his fingers tighten on her flesh a little.

"Not…not in here, either," she said in a sudden panic.

''Absolutely not,'' Richard returned, and indicated the security camera up in the corner.

She stared at him as he went about inserting his security key-card, her eyes widening when he pressed the penthouse floor.

''You live in the penthouse?''

''One of them. There are two in this building.''

My God. A penthouse. She would never have thought Richard a penthouse type of man. It seemed he'd been right when he'd said earlier tonight that she didn't know him very well.

The lift started to rise so smoothly she was barely aware of movement. Holly hadn't taken much notice of her surrounds on the short drive here. She'd been too worked up with a distracting mixture of nerves and excitement.

In truth, she hadn't needed to see where they were going. She already knew Richard had recently bought an apartment on a point at East Balmain, not far from the Diamonds. He'd told her so.

He hadn't told her it was a penthouse, however.

Would a man planning to remarry buy a penthouse to live in? A penthouse was more of a bachelor playground, a place for girlfriends and mistresses, not wives. Good Lord, maybe Richard was planning to set her up as his mistress! Maybe he already had some other woman lined up to be his wife.

The lift eased to a supersmooth halt before the door whooshed open and Holly gasped. For straight ahead, across an expanse of shiny marble floor, was a huge window that had the most spectacular night-time view, with the bridge on the right and the skyscrapers of North Sydney straight ahead. As she walked towards it the harbour below came more into view, the reflection of lights dancing in the darkened waters.

"In here, Holly."

She whirled to find that Richard had opened a door she hadn't noticed. She saw then that there was another door in the wall opposite, clearly the entry to the second penthouse.

Holly walked into Richard's penthouse, expecting one thing but being confronted with something totally different.

"Oh!" she said with surprise as she glanced around.

"What were you expecting? Black leather and bear rugs?"

"Something like that."

"Are you disappointed?"

"Heavens, no. It's…fantastic. Nothing like a penthouse at all. More like a holiday house," she said as she walked slowly around the open-plan living areas, admiring the easy living layout and the relaxed furniture.

"I'll give you a grand tour in the morning," Richard said, and started coming towards her across the blue-and-yellow rug she was standing on. "For now, the only room I want to show you is my bedroom."

All the breath zoomed from Holly's lungs as he pulled her into his arms.

"Can I kiss you now?" he asked, his voice soft but his eyes hard. So was his body.

Holly was seized by a mad, mischievous moment. "What if I said no?"

His eyes made her shiver.

"Don't tease me, Holly. I'm not in the mood for games."

His mouth closed off any further conversation. His arms encircled her back, his hands settling at opposite ends of her spine, his huge palms keeping her pressed against the full length of him.

She'd known he was a big man. A powerful man. Now she felt his power, and his passion, his kiss going on and on and on. His head didn't lift till she was dizzy from lack of air.

His sweeping her up into his arms was a welcome move. It saved her from falling. As he carried her from the living room down a long hallway she buried her face into his chest, trying desperately not to think, or worry.

Strangely, this time, his kiss hadn't totally addled her brains. Maybe because she knew the moment of truth was at hand. The mind was a terrible thing. Cruel and merciless. And sometimes perverse.

By the time Richard carried her through an open doorway into what was obviously the master bedroom, the butterflies in Holly's stomach had reached epidemic proportions. Her head lifted from his chest and darted nervously to the bed, which was huge, with a white cane headboard and a shiny blue satin quilt.

Holly took some comfort from the fact that it was at least a new bed. No way did she want to share some bed with Richard that Joanna had slept in. Which was pretty silly, really. What did it matter? Alanna was right. Jealousy was a curse.

But she couldn't seem to help it. She was jealous

of Richard's love for his beautiful wife. And fearful that *she* could never measure up, either in bed or out.

He lowered her down, down onto the satin quilt, pressing light kisses to her mouth all the while, nothing like the wildly hungry kiss he'd given her in the living room. It seemed that, now he had her in his bedroom, he didn't want to hurry. He wanted to savour the moment. Savour her.

For a minute or so he kept her captive under his mouth, but then he rolled onto his side next to her, propping himself up on one elbow whilst his free hand began to explore her body.

At last her mind was merciful, spinning her out into another world where she no longer worried about her own performance. Her focus was all on what Richard was doing to her and the wonderful ways her body kept responding, as though it had been waiting for him to come along to show her what she was capable of feeling. When he slipped his hand in over her right breast, the nipple became even more erect. When his outstretched palm slid back and forth over it, everything inside her contracted fiercely.

She moaned with the exquisite pleasure of it all, and the desire for more. Much more.

"As delicious as this dress is," he murmured, taking his hand away, "it has to go. But first, this very sexy belt."

The belt was not unlike a large silver watchband that expanded and contracted. Its clasp was strong, but very simple to undo.

"Interesting," he said as he slid the belt from her waist, placing it beside him on the bed before returning his attention to the dress. He quickly found the clasp that anchored the halter around her neck, unsnapping it, then peeling the top down over her breasts.

''Beautiful,'' he murmured, and bent his mouth to the same nipple he'd been playing with, licking it at first, then nipping it with his teeth before sucking it deep into his mouth.

Holly moaned again, the sensations of his suckling seeming to have some secret connection to that area between her legs. When his lips tugged on her breast there was a corresponding tug down there. No, not a tug. An exciting tightening. She didn't want him to ever stop.

He did stop, but not for long, his mouth moving over to her other breast whilst his right hand took possession of the bereft nipple, squeezing it quite hard.

She cried out, writhing against the rather confusing combination of pleasure and pain. Did she like it, or not?

He took an agonisingly long time before releasing her burning nipple, yet as soon as he did she wanted him to do it again. He obliged, and when his head finally lifted his normally cold eyes blazed down at her like molten steel.

Lord knew what she looked like. Her face felt hot and her heart was going so fast she could very well be heading for a coronary. Her mouth fell open and she was panting like a marathon runner on a hot day.

His stripping her of the rest of the dress was achieved with considerable speed, along with the removal of her white satin G-string. He left her silver high heels on, however, then stunned her by picking up the silver belt and refastening it around her naked waist.

"The chains of love," he said, his hand sliding down over her stomach and between her legs.

His fingers on her breast had made her writhe. His fingers inside her body propelled her to a place infinitely more intense, a place she'd never been to before. Any pleasure seemed overlaid with an agitating tension that made her grimace and groan. She wanted to tell him to stop. But she couldn't, and he didn't.

Holly came with a rush, a cry bursting from her lips as she was propelled headlong into her first full-blown orgasm. She squeezed her eyes tightly shut, wallowing in the pleasure as her flesh spasmed over and over.

So this was what it was like. No wonder people became addicted to the experience.

Finally, the contractions stopped, followed up by the most delicious feeling of abandonment.

Richard's hand did not abandon her, however, Holly's eyes flying open on a gasp when it continued to probe and to play with her down there, even more intimately. At first, she wasn't sure if she wanted him to, but he must have known what he was doing, because eventually her first climax became a dim memory and she began craving another. Quite desperately.

When her hips started to lift from the bed, he did abandon her. Totally.

"Wh...where are you going?" she cried when he rose from the bed.

"Not very far," he returned, his eyes remaining hot on her as he began to strip off his own clothes.

Holly didn't know whose gaze was more intense.

His or hers. She could not believe how magnificent his body was. Clearly, he worked out a lot.

He seemed to like her shape as well.

"You look incredibly sexy with that belt on," he said.

She flushed wildly, having forgotten about the belt. A downwards glance reminded her of what he'd said when he'd put it back on her.

The chains of love.

Holly didn't think it was love making Richard look at her the way he was looking at her. She suspected it didn't have much to do with her own feelings at that moment, either.

All she cared about was having Richard back on this bed with her. And soon.

When he yanked open the top drawer of his bedside chest and picked up a box of condoms, Holly blinked. Having that much protection on hand was hardly the act of a man who hadn't looked at a woman in the last eighteen months. Richard's mother didn't know him any better than *she* did.

But Holly was beyond caring at this moment. Desire had a very narrow focus.

"You don't need to use protection," she blurted out. "Not unless you think it's necessary. I...I'm on the pill."

"You're not at any risk from me," he reassured her as he tossed the box back into the drawer and pushed it shut.

"Don't...don't you think I'd better take these shoes off?" she said when he went to climb back on the bed. "They have very sharp heels."

''If you like. But not the belt. The belt stays. No, let me...''

She gasped when he took her by the ankles and pulled her crossways on the bed. He removed the left shoe first, dropping it onto the floor before bending her knee up and placing the sole of her foot flat on the edge of the bed. Then he did the same thing with her right foot, placing it so that her legs were far enough apart for him to see every secret, glistening part of her.

Her heart started thudding as he stared down at her. One part of her wanted to close her legs. But it was not the strongest part.

Finally, he came forward to kneel between her legs, his hands reaching to run up and down the front of her thighs. Her belly tightened, then trembled. Heat flooded her face as he continued to stare at her down there.

''Don't,'' she choked out. ''Don't look at me like that.''

''I want to look at you like that. I like seeing how much you want me. You do want me, Holly, don't you?''

''You know I do,'' she cried, shaken by the force of her wanting. ''Oh, please...don't tease me, Richard.''

''Tell me what you want.''

''Just you.''

''So easily pleased,'' he muttered, then did what she craved, entering her with a single, forceful thrust.

Her mouth fell open on a raw cry, her buttocks contracting fiercely. He scooped them up high with his hands and began driving into her with a long, slow, relentless rhythm, his eyes narrowing on hers as he did so.

''Oh, God,'' she gasped.

Her head began to twist from side to side on the bed, her eyes squeezing shut in an effort to hide the wild pleasure in them.

''No, don't close your eyes,'' he commanded gruffly. ''Open them. Look at me!''

She opened them and stared up at him.

Did he want to watch her climax? Or did he want her to watch *him* climax?

Both prospects excited her.

What kind of girl was she to like lovemaking like this?

''Stop thinking,'' he ordered her. Then, before she could protest, he rolled over onto his back, taking her with him, like a yacht tossed in a storm. Suddenly, she was on top of him, swaying like a mast.

Her knees dug into the mattress on each side of him to steady herself, the action automatically lifting her hips, her internal muscles contracting to stop him from slipping out of her body. He grunted, then pulled her down hard onto him so that he was buried inside her to the hilt.

Holly blushed when he reached for her breasts, which were oh, so accessible to him now.

''No need for you to be shy,'' he said as he stroked his hands down over her breasts, each action ending with a tug on her nipples. ''You have truly magnificent breasts,'' he said in a desire-thickened voice, doing the same action over and over, each tug on her nipples pulling her forward till she was leaning over him, her breasts dangling close to his lips, her nipples harder than they had ever been.

"Put one in my mouth."

His erotic request evoked another flood of heat in Holly. But there was no thought of denying him. Unlike with Dave, she didn't feel Richard was lying to her when he complimented her body. His eyes reflected true admiration as he touched her. True excitement, too. His flesh felt even fuller inside her. Harder. Thicker.

When she directed one of the aching nipples between his lips, he drew the whole aureole into his mouth, sucking on it and playing with her at the same time. Not her other breast this time, but her buttocks, stroking them, then cupping them, lifting her bottom up and down, up and down, up and down.

Holly's moans reflected the sensations that began bombarding her body.

As much as she wanted to please Richard, it wasn't long before she needed to sit up, to ride him, to pursue release from the tortuous feelings building up within her belly. Her pleasure had turned dark, and desperate.

Wrenching her breast out of his mouth, she began to ride him, quite frantically. She was dimly aware of his hands grabbing her hips, of his urging her on, of his hot hungry words of encouragement.

But she didn't really need any help. She was now in command of the situation. In control. No, not in control, she thought with a hint of hysteria when her hair fell down and her mouth fell open.

He came before her, but it was only a matter of a few seconds. Perhaps his release triggered hers.

Whatever, the sensation of coming with Richard deep inside her blew Holly away. She could not get over the way he felt, the way *she* felt. Even before her contractions began to fade she knew she could never walk away from Richard after this. She would be whatever he wanted her to be. Girlfriend. Mistress. Wife.

Slave.

''Oh, God,'' she cried as she collapsed across his chest, unable to stay upright any longer.

Another ragged sigh puffed from her lungs.

''Is that a good sigh or a bad sigh?'' he asked softly.

She didn't lift her head or answer him for a while, amazed to find that, once her orgasm was totally over, some common sense came back.

''Holly?''

She dragged her head up a few inches, pushing her hair out of her face at the same time. ''Don't be silly. How could it be a bad sigh? That was incredible.''

''*You* were incredible,'' he said, looping her hair behind her ears for her.

''I...I'm not normally like that,'' she said truthfully, putting her head back down on his chest.

''Maybe it's this belt,'' he murmured, stroking down her back till he reached it. He began rubbing his hand back and forth across the links, touching her skin at the same time, making her break out into goose-bumps.

''Maybe,'' she said with a shiver.

''In that case, you're not allowed to take it off tonight,'' he said. ''In fact, you have to keep it on all weekend.''

Holly's head jerked up. "What do you mean, all weekend?"

"You don't honestly think I'm going to let you go home in the morning, do you? Not after that performance just now. You're going to stay here. With me. Till I take you home Monday morning."

"But..."

"No buts. And no clothes. Just that belt, and wall-to-wall sex."

She blushed wildly, both shamed and excited by what he was proposing.

"But for now," he swept on, "I think it's time for a shower together. Or would you prefer a bath? You choose."

She stared up at him.

You choose.

Such a simple choice, really. But either answer carried potential danger. Holly wasn't the sort of girl who could separate sex and love indefinitely.

He'd called the belt around her waist the chains of love. If she wore it for him all weekend—and nothing else—the chains of love would surely slip around her heart.

Holly wasn't sure what Richard wanted from her ultimately, but she knew one thing. Love wasn't on *his* agenda.

If only he hadn't chosen that moment to withdraw from her body, showing her what her world would be like without him.

"Come along," he said, and scooped her up out of the bed. "I can see I will have to make all the decisions where you're concerned."

Holly didn't like the sound of that. If she was going to be weak, she was going to be weak on her terms.

"A shower," she pronounced as he carried her into the all blue bathroom. "And this belt comes off first."

He ground to halt. "Why? I like it on you."

So did she. Too much.

"It's only cheap silver plating," she told him as she struggled to unhook it. "It might tarnish if it gets wet."

"I'll buy you a new one if it does," he pronounced, then carried her, belt and all, into the shower.

CHAPTER TEN

HOLLY woke with her silver belt still encircling her waist, and Richard's hand over her right breast. Fortunately, he was sound asleep. Totally dead to the world.

As well he should be, she thought with remembered awe as she very carefully lifted his hand off her breast, placed it palm down on the mattress, then slid out from under the sheets.

She'd been spot on when she'd said he would be good at everything. But he wasn't just good at sex. He was absolutely fabulous. He also had amazing stamina. My God, anyone would think he *hadn't* had sex in yonks. She couldn't count the number of times he'd made love to her. And not in the same way twice!

She now knew he was also a good kisser in places she'd never imagined being kissed before. She'd also been educated in a couple of positions she had never tried before.

Holly shook her head as she tiptoed into the bathroom. Even before she shut the door behind her, the memories of what had happened in there flooded back. Richard hadn't been the only one last night who'd surprised her. Her own sexual shenanigans had been wickedly uncharacteristic.

She'd been more than willing to use her hands on

him, and her mouth. And very happy to lean wantonly back against the tiles whilst he'd returned the favour.

Holly shivered at the memory.

When she returned to the bedroom and glanced at his gloriously naked form once more, Richard's proposal for the rest of this weekend swirled back into her mind.

"No buts. And no clothes," he'd said. "Just that belt, and wall-to-wall sex."

God, but she was tempted. Just the thought turned her on.

But to *really* do that, to walk around Richard's penthouse in the nude all day, to obey his every sexual command, was simply not on. It was not only shaming but demeaning. She would not do it.

Holly twisted the corrupting belt around so that the clasp was at the front. Her hands actually shook as she unclipped it, as though they didn't want to obey her, but once they did a huge sigh of relief rippled through her.

Next, she looked for something to put on, shuddering when she spotted her pink dress on the floor, along with her panties and shoes.

No way would she be putting those on, either.

She had noticed a robe hanging up on the back of the bathroom door, but that had to be the one Richard was currently using. She quickly found the door that led into his walk-in closet and started searching for a spare robe, or something suitable to put on after she had a shower.

Everything in there was very neat and organised, just as she would imagine Richard's wardrobe to be. All his suits were hanging up neatly in a row, along with a large number of business shirts. All white or blue. Along the opposite wall was a long row of casual clothes. Trousers, shirts, tops and jackets of all kinds, even leather.

But there were no spare robes.

After dithering for a while, Holly went back to his business shirts and selected a blue one. It was very good material, she noted. Soft and uncreasable. Expensive. Of course the darned thing would swim on her, but that was okay. She wanted to be well covered up when Richard woke.

Taking the shirt with her, she tiptoed back to the bathroom.

Richard woke to the sound of the shower running.

He smiled as he stretched. God, but he felt marvellous. Last night was exactly what he'd needed.

Holly was what he'd needed. Not just for one night, either. Or even one weekend. It might be a bit too soon to propose marriage, but there was no reason why he couldn't ask her to move in with him. When the flower shop sold, she'd have to find somewhere else to live. Why not here, with him?

How wonderful it would be to come home to Holly every night. The memory of what she'd done to him in the shower popped back into his mind, making his flesh twitch back to life. She'd proved to be somewhat more experienced, sexually, than he'd imagined, but he'd surprised her, too, a few times. He was sure of it.

Still, she'd wanted him as much and as often as he'd wanted her. Hopefully, by the end of this weekend, she'd be more than willing to do *whatever* he wanted.

Unfortunately, her flower shop probably wouldn't sell for ages. Property in Sydney was proving hard to shift at the moment. Maybe he could help things along.

Richard was planning a rather ruthless move on his part when the phone rang.

He wondered who it could be, calling him this early on a Sunday morning. A glance at his watch showed it was only twenty past nine.

Richard leant over and swept the phone off its cradle.

''Richard Crawford,'' he answered crisply.

''Richard, it's Reece.''

''Reece! Now what are you doing up at this hour? I thought you and Alanna would sleep in till noon at least. You—''

''Is Holly there with you?'' Reece cut in brusquely.

''Er…she's in the shower.''

''I think you might have a problem.''

Richard's stomach tightened. ''What kind of problem?''

''You know how you told me at the party last night that Holly wasn't from Wives Wanted.''

''Yes…''

''It's a pity you didn't tell me that earlier.''

''What do you mean?''

''When you rang Alanna earlier this week to say that you were bringing a date to our party, she assumed she would be one of Natalie's girls.''

Richard sucked in sharply. ''You *told* Alanna I signed up with Wives Wanted?''

"Sorry, mate. There didn't seem any reason not to tell her, considering *she* was one of Natalie's girls."

"I guess not. So what are you saying? That Alanna said something to Holly? She told her that I'd been looking for a wife through an introduction agency?"

"Afraid so. When they were in the powder room together. Alanna said Holly seemed okay about it, other than being somewhat surprised. Anyway, the girls promised each other not to say anything to either of us last night. They were worried we might be angry. But this morning, Alanna decided you should know that Holly knows. She also said you should know that Holly said she would never marry without love, especially a man who was still in love with his dead wife."

Richard clenched his teeth. He wasn't still in love with Joanna. He hated her. But he supposed his hate was just as much of an impediment to falling in love again. Once bitten that badly, a million times shy.

"I see," he said, his brain ticking away with the implications of what Reece had just told him. At least this news explained why Holly had become stroppy with him at the party for a while.

But she'd still come home with him, hadn't she? And still gone to bed with him.

That said a lot in his favour.

"You could lie to her, of course, Richard. Tell her you love her. Tell her you're totally over Joanna. Lots of women will believe whatever they want to believe."

"I won't do that, Reece. Did *you* tell *Alanna* you loved her?"

"No, but then Alanna's a very unusual woman. She

doesn't want to be loved. She's even more pragmatic than I am. But blind Freddy can see that your Holly is nothing like us. She's quite young, for starters. And idealistic. A bit like you used to be. I wasn't keen on your going to Wives Wanted to find a wife. Most of those women on that database are out for what they can get. But I still think you might have pulled the wrong straw with Holly.''

''I don't think so. She's what I want. And I mean to have her, one way or the other.''

''You've already had her, mate, by the sounds of things. That doesn't mean you have to marry her.''

''I know that, Reece. But I'm going to, if she'll have me.''

''What will you do about the Wives Wanted business?''

''The only thing I can do. Tell Holly everything, of course.''

Up to a point. He wasn't about to spill his guts over what Joanna had done to him. He would concentrate on his need to move on with his life, the same way Holly was moving on with hers. Why not move on together? he would argue. They liked each other and desired each other. He would also tell her he thought she'd make a wonderful wife and mother. It wasn't flattery. It was the truth.

''Thanks for telling me, Reece,'' Richard said. ''I appreciate it. And tell Alanna not to worry. Everything will be fine.''

''I hope so.''

''I'd better go. The water went off in the shower some time ago. She'll be coming out of the bathroom any time now.''

He hung up just in time. Holly emerged, her hair down and damp, her face scrubbed of make-up, her beautiful body totally covered by one of his blue business shirts.

For all that, she looked incredibly sexy.

When she saw that he was awake, she halted with a small gasp, a delightful pink zooming into her cheeks.

Richard smiled, thinking how nice it was that she was susceptible to some ''morning after'' embarrassment, that she wasn't the kind of girl who was totally blasé about getting up to what they'd got up to last night.

''And good morning to you, too,'' he said softly. ''You're wearing one of my shirts, I see.''

He loved the way her blush was quickly replaced by a saucy toss of her head. She had spirit, this girl he'd chosen to marry.

''You didn't honestly think I was going to go around with no clothes on today, did you? Or wear that silly belt.''

His dark brows lifted. He'd actually forgotten about saying that. ''A man can always hope.''

''Sorry,'' she said with a haughty sniff. ''If you want a sex slave, you'll have to go elsewhere.''

He had to laugh. ''You are unique, Holly, I'll give you that. And intriguingly unpredictable. After last night a man could be forgiven for thinking you might have enjoyed acting out the sex-slave fantasy.''

''Well, you'd be wrong.''

''I often am,'' he said. ''Especially about you. So what's on the agenda for today? I am yours to command.''

She rolled her eyes. ''Very funny. You might be a man of leisure today but I have to go home. I always do the books on a Sunday.''

''You will not be doing the books today, madam,'' Richard said sternly. ''Or any other Sunday, for that matter. Let your stepmother do them. Or let her pay for an accountant.''

''You're right. I'm mad. No more books. In that case, I suppose you could take me out to brunch somewhere. I'm hungry as a horse. But you'll have to drive me home first. I will need to change.''

''Oh, I don't know. You look very fetching, dressed like that. Alternatively, we could eat in. I could go get us some videos and a pizza.''

Already, Richard was changing his mind about bringing up the subject of Wives Wanted today. Why spoil the moment?

''Not on your life!'' she retorted. ''I spent twelve months having pizzas and videos every weekend. And paying for them myself. I wouldn't let you buy me a dress, but I don't mind you paying to take me somewhere nice to eat. That's perfectly acceptable.''

Richard could see she wasn't going to let him drag her back to bed for the rest of the day, damn it. If he was going to get up and take her out somewhere, he might as well clear the air on the subject of the Wives Wanted agency right here and now.

''Somewhere nice it will be, then. But before I get dressed and run you home,'' he said, ''could you come over here and sit down on the bed next to me?'' He patted the side of the bed with one hand as he dragged a sheet over his lower half with the other. ''I have something I want to discuss with you.''

''What?'' she asked a bit nervously as she did as he asked. But as she sat down and crossed her legs his shirt parted across her thighs and he had a tantalising glimpse of the dark triangle of curly hair that arrowed down between her legs.

''I've just had a call from Reece,'' he said before he succumbed to temptation and pulled her into the bed with him.

''Oh?'' Her hand lifted to finger-comb her hair back from her forehead.

''Alanna told him what she'd said to you in the powder room last night.''

''Oh!''

Was that alarm in her eyes?

Damn it all, but she could be hard to read at times.

''Why didn't you mention it last night?'' he asked, watching her face closely.

Definite guilt in her eyes this time. Though Lord knew what she had to feel guilty about.

''I...I didn't want to spoil anything,'' she said.

Aaah, now he got it. She'd wanted him to bring her home and make love to her. That had been her priority at the time.

''But you were still angry with me,'' he pointed out.

''Not really. More like...bewildered. I...I couldn't understand why you would want to go to that kind of agency, or why you would think you had to buy yourself a wife, the way Reece did.''

''Reece didn't buy Alanna.''

''Oh, come now, Richard. Do you think she'd have married him if he'd been poor?''

''No. But Reece's wealth was not the whole picture. They connected straight away. And the chemistry was right. The way we did.''

Now she definitely looked alarmed. Or was it shock?

''What is it you're saying, Richard? Surely you're not asking *me* to marry you?''

''Would that be so surprising?''

''Yes! I mean...I thought...I just...I... For pity's sake, we've only known each other a little over a week. And please don't go saying you've fallen madly in love with me.''

''I don't intend to,'' he said, and watched her eyes widen.

''Wow. You can be brutally honest when you want to be, can't you?''

''Would you prefer I did a Dave on you?''

''Lord, no,'' she said with a shudder.

''In that case, hear me out,'' he said, throwing back the sheet and climbing out of the bed. ''Wait here.''

Holly remained rooted to the spot, her head spinning. So he *had* been targeting her as a marital candidate.

Holly couldn't deny she felt flattered, but, goodness, what was the rush? It couldn't be because he wanted sex. She'd slept with him last night and would undoubtedly sleep with him again, whenever he wanted. Her insistence earlier that she wouldn't be his sex slave was just so much rubbish. Being Richard's sex slave was exactly what Holly would like to be.

But his wife?

No, thank you very much. She might have toyed with the idea last night, when she'd been turned on to the max. But the cold light of morning had a way of making her see common sense.

Holly refused to play second fiddle in any man's life! If and when she got married, she definitely wanted a man who was in love with her. A deep and everlasting love. She deserved to be loved and was not going to settle for anything less!

The bathroom door opened and out he came.

Thank God, he'd put something on. Though what he was wearing wasn't much of a covering, the navy silk robe only loosely sashed around his hips. Most of his massive chest was on display, the matted curls in the centre giving him a cavemanish look. Adding to his primal appearance was his stubbly chin and his slightly messy hair.

"Come with me," he said, taking her by the hand.

"Where are wc going?" she asked as he practically dragged her along the hallway.

"My study," he answered.

The room he took her into was nothing like his father's study back at Strathfield. Bright and sunny, the walls were a pale yellow, the floor covered in the same cream tiles that seemed to run through the whole penthouse. One wall was almost entirely of glass, with sliding doors leading out onto a huge terrace. Another wall had built-in shelves, housing a colourful array of books. A blue-and-yellow rug stretched out in front of the desk, which was sleek and modern. The desktop was clear, she noted, except for a phone and a laptop.

"Sit," Richard said, and indicated the blue office chair behind the desk.

She sat, wondering what on earth he was about to

show her. Richard grabbed the arm of the chair and pulled it down in front of the laptop. He stayed standing next to her and started clicking the mouse. In no time, he'd brought up a photograph of a brunette who would have given Catherine Zeta-Jones a run for her money.

"She was the first woman from Wives Wanted I took out," he said. "She's a television producer. Thirty-four and divorced."

He clicked up another raven-haired beauty.

"Took her out next," Richard said. "She's a pathologist. Thirty-five. Never been married."

Two more stunning brunettes filled the screen with successive clicks, each one accompanied by a succinct report from Richard. Each one had higher education, as well as incredible physical beauty.

At last he switched the computer off, pushed it over a little and perched on the edge of the desk, facing her.

"To answer your first question, you wondered why I would go to such an agency. I'll tell you why. I'm thirty-eight years old, Holly. I've been in love, I've been married and I've been horribly hurt. For eighteen months I could hardly bear to go out, let alone date. But life does move on and the time came when I wanted a woman in my life, and in my bed again. As well as that, I want a child. And not when I'm in my dotage."

Holly sat up straighter in the chair. A *child*! So that was the reason behind his urgency. Now why hadn't she thought of that?

"I know people have children all the time these days out of wedlock," he went on, "but that's not me. I wanted my child to be legitimate. And I wanted a wife for myself, too. I'd been lonely and celibate for long enough. But I couldn't see myself cruising singles bars every weekend, or signing up for speed-dating night."

"But don't you meet a lot of women at work, and in the course of your social life? A man in your position would go to lots of dos."

"Like I said, I'm thirty-eight. Most of the women around my age that I meet are married, or divorced. The married ones are out of bounds and the divorced ones are carrying too much emotional baggage for me. I have enough of my own. I saw how successful Reece's marriage was using Wives Wanted and I thought, Why not give it a try?"

Now that she had heard his explanation, Holly could see it was reasonable.

"So what happened?" she probed.

"It didn't work out."

"But all those women were incredible. And brilliant!"

"Gold diggers, every one of them."

"How do you know that?"

"Trust me," he said drily.

"But isn't financial security part of the deal?"

"I guess so. But I suspect Reece was very lucky, to find a real diamond amongst the paste jewels on offer."

"But they were all very beautiful."

"In a skin-deep fashion."

"Did...did you sleep with any of them?"

Holly hated herself for asking, but she had to know.

"Not a one. There was no chemistry. Not for me,

anyway. Every one of them left me cold. You, however, my sweet darling Holly,'' he said, yanking the chair up between his legs, ''you heated my blood from the first moment I saw you.''

Holly was already melting from his endearment when he cupped her face and bent down to kiss her.

Not a hard kiss. Or a hungry one. A soft, tender, loving kiss that rocked her soul, and her belief that she had not fallen in love with Richard.

What a fool she was. A silly fool. Didn't she know she'd been half in love with him before she'd even met him? He was everything she'd ever wanted in a man. The trouble was, as perfect as he was in her eyes, in his heart of hearts he would always belong to someone else.

Tears pricked at her eyes, bringing panic. She didn't want him to know how she felt about him. And he might add two and two together, if she started crying. He might use the knowledge against her. Make her do things she knew she shouldn't do, like say yes to marrying him.

So she cupped *his* face with her hand and deepened the kiss, all to hide her tears. He slid off the desk and pulled her up out of the chair at the same time, yanking her hard against him.

Their mouths burst apart and he glared down at her.

''You shouldn't have done that,'' he growled.

''Why not?''

''Because I've been wanting to do this ever since I woke up.''

He wrenched his robe apart before his hands scooped up under his blue shirt, spanning her waist and squeezing tightly, rather like the silver belt had done. She gasped when he lifted her and sat her on the edge of the desk. Moaned when he pushed her legs wide. Cried out when he plunged into her.

None of their matings the previous night had been anything like this. This was wild and primitive. The sounds they both made. The lack of finesse. The roughness of it all.

He came quickly, his back arching, his mouth falling wide with a primal cry as his flesh exploded inside hers. Holly could not believe it when her body swiftly followed with a climax just as intense. She clutched at his shoulders, sobbing as the spasms twisted at her insides.

He swore and scooped her up off the desk, holding her close. Her legs automatically wrapped around his hips, her arms around his back.

''Sorry,'' he muttered. ''Sorry.''

She buried her face into his chest and surrendered to the need to weep.

''I'll take you home now,'' he said gently when she finally quietened.

''Yes, please,'' she said, feeling calmer. And resigned.

So she loved him. There wasn't much Holly could do about that.

She would undoubtedly continue to go out with him. And sleep with him. But she would not—absolutely not—agree to marry him!

''Do you still want me to take you somewhere nice to eat?''

No use pretending she didn't. So she nodded and he smiled, and her fate was sealed.

CHAPTER ELEVEN

"RICHARD! So it *is* you!"

Richard knew the identity of the woman before he lifted his eyes from the chicken and mushroom risotto he'd been thoroughly enjoying.

It had been a mistake, he accepted as he finally looked up, to bring Holly to one of the trendy eating places he and Joanna used to frequent. Despite the time lapse, he should have realised that some of his wife's old crowd might still go to their regular haunts. The Cockle Bay Wharf at Darling Harbour was a favourite of the rich and idle on a Sunday summer's afternoon.

"Hello, Kim," he said.

Of all Joanna's girlfriends, Kim was probably her closest. She'd been the chief bridesmaid at their wedding. Richard had quite liked her to begin with. Most of Joanna's friends were of the bright, bubbly kind. Good fun to be with. But he'd changed his mind when she'd made a serious play for him one night, uncaring that she'd been in her best friend's home, or that her own husband had been just a room away.

Since then, she had divorced that particular husband, after he'd served his purpose, of course, which was to provide her with an income for life. Kim was a bitch through and through. A beautiful bitch, though.

Birds of a feather, he now realised.

''It's great to see you out and about again,'' she gushed. ''And looking so trendy! Do you know I was with Joanna when she bought you that outfit. It suits you, darling. There again, Joanna's taste was impeccable, especially in men. But I am blathering on, aren't I? Would you and your little friend like to join us? We're just sitting over there.'' And she indicated a long table full of people across the way. Richard glanced over but didn't recognise anyone else from his past life.

''Holly's not my little friend,'' Richard informed her coolly. ''She's my girlfriend. And, no, thank you, Kim, we'd prefer to be alone.''

''How romantic. There again, you always were a romantic, Richard. We'll catch up some other time, shall we?'' she said, and actually had the temerity to bend and kiss him on the cheek before undulating off back to her companions.

Richard felt as if his face were suddenly carved in ice.

Poor Holly was not looking too comfortable, either.

Damn Kim for going on about Joanna and the stupid clothes he was wearing. He'd only put them on because Holly had picked them out of his wardrobe, not because Joanna had bought them for him.

But Holly wouldn't believe that now. Which was a shame.

Less than five minutes earlier, he'd been thinking how happy she looked sitting there in her simple but very pretty lemon sundress, her skin glowing and her long brown hair gleaming in the sunshine.

''Sorry about that,'' he said abruptly. ''Kim's an old friend of my wife's. Her best friend, actually.''

Even as he said the words, a thought occurred to him. Kim would probably know the truth about Joanna. Female friends always confided in each other. But how much did she know, exactly?

Richard decided he would ask, as soon as he got the chance. He probably wouldn't like the answers but he had to know. Had to put the past behind him once and for all.

Till then, he wasn't going to let the memory of his wife, or her so-called friends, spoil his afternoon with Holly.

And it could, if the frown on her face was anything to go by.

"I'm not upset, if that's what you're thinking," he said.

Holly stared at him across the table. Who did he think he was kidding?

She'd been flattered by the way he'd set Kim straight about her status in his life. Holly had taken an instant dislike to the woman. Maybe because she was drop-dead gorgeous, one of those slim, cool blondes who always looked as if they'd just stepped out of a beauty salon.

But anyone with half a brain could see that Richard running into his wife's best friend had thrown a dampener over proceedings.

His eyes, which had been bright and sparkly all day, were now the colour of a wintry lake under a cloudy sky. The muscles around his jaw looked stiff and his mouth was pressed into a thin, hard line.

He certainly hadn't got over his wife. Not in the slightest. His mother had been right. Any last lingering hope that some miracle might happen and Richard might fall in love with *her* eventually went straight down the gurgler.

Holly's dismay was acute, and telling. She was setting herself up for another personal disaster with this man. One far worse than Dave, because this time she was going into things with her eyes well and truly open.

Richard didn't love her. He would *never* love her.

Face it, Holly, and deal with it.

Facing it was very depressing. Dealing with it quite impossible. Because she could not walk away from him. She loved him.

''Thank you for calling me your girlfriend,'' she said, trying her best not to sound the way she was suddenly feeling.

''I would have preferred to say fiancée,'' he returned.

She stared at him, then shook her head. ''Please don't.''

''Please don't what?''

''Don't keep on about that. I'm happy to be your girlfriend, Richard. But I won't marry you.''

''You know, Holly, it's only in the western culture that people marry for love. Romance is all very nice, but it's not all that reliable. Look at our divorce rate. Most of those couples thought they were in love when they tied the knot. Being *in love* doesn't last. Caring and commitment are what makes a marriage last. That, and common goals. And children. You want children, don't you?''

''Yes, of course I do.''

''There is no *of course* about it. Some women these

days don't want children. And lots of men, according to the ladies from Wives Wanted. I will give you children, plus the security to raise them right. I will also give you caring and commitment. If this weekend is anything to go by you won't have any complaints about our sex life, either. Our compatibility in bed is better than lots of people who are in love."

Holly sighed. "That all sounds very reasonable, Richard, but you don't *love* me. I'm all alone in the world. My parents are gone. So are my grandparents. I have an aunt in Melbourne I might have seen three times in my lifetime. And a gay uncle who moved to San Francisco when I was a teenager. That's it. I have no family who loves me. I *need* to be loved by my husband."

"That's romantic ideology," he said sharply. "What a wife and mother needs is a husband who can provide and protect you and yours. Who will always be faithful. Who will never deliberately hurt you or let you down. I will deliver all that, Holly. I give you my solemn word."

His eyes bored into Holly's, the passion in his voice making her doubt her resolve to resist his proposal. Maybe he was right. Maybe they could be happy together.

But then she remembered that photo of Joanna, which she had seen propped up against her coffin.

She would always be there, coming between them. The beautiful first wife. The love of Richard's life.

"Just think about it," he went on. "That's all I ask."

"All right," she agreed, knowing she would probably think about little else.

''Shall we go?'' he suggested.

''Why not?'' They'd eaten most of their risotto and drunk all of the excellent bottle of white wine Richard had ordered with it.

Richard called for the bill.

Five minutes later they were strolling across the old iron bridge that took them to the other side of Darling Harbour, her hand enclosed tightly in Richard's. They hadn't spoken since they'd got up from the table.

''Would you like to go into the casino?'' he asked.

''Would you?'' she countered, glancing up at the Star City complex.

''Not particularly. I'm not a gambler. I have a bet on the Melbourne Cup each year but that's about it.''

''I have a flutter on that as well. But I never win.''

He smiled. ''Neither do I. What shall we do, then?''

''Whatever you like,'' she returned, perhaps a little thoughtlessly. Her mind was just so full with tortured thoughts.

''Right. See that taxi rank over there? Let's go!''

They hadn't driven here. They'd taken a taxi, Richard explaining that parking at Darling Harbour on a Sunday afternoon was difficult.

''Where are you taking me?'' she asked breathlessly as he pulled her along the pavement at power-walking pace.

''Where do you think?''

Holly ground to a halt once she realised what he was talking about.

''No,'' she said, panic-stricken at the idea of going back to that penthouse and being seduced over and over. Her mind was already in a mess. "I don't want to do that, Richard."

His eyes bored into hers. "Yes, you do."

"Well, yes, I do, but I'm not going to. You don't understand. I…I've never experienced anything like I experienced with you last night. And again this morning. It's sent me into a tail-spin."

"What's wrong with my making love to you?"

"It's confusing. And corrupting. I mean…I know you might laugh at this, but I…I've never had an orgasm before. Then, in the space of a few hours I had about twenty. With you."

He just stared at her. "Are you serious?"

"Of course I'm serious! Why would I lie about something as embarrassing as that?"

His eyes softened on her. "I don't think that's an embarrassing admission at all. I think it's sweet. You're sweet."

"I'm a silly, naïve little fool!" she snapped.

"No. Not at all. You just haven't had the right lovers. I'm flattered that I gave you such pleasure. But why not have more where that came from?"

"I knew you'd say something like that. I should never have told you. I *am* a fool."

"Would all women be such fools, then," he muttered. "Okay, I'll take you home, if that's what you want. But I'll be over to visit you tomorrow night."

"Tomorrow's one of my gym nights."

"Then cancel it."

"No."

"There's a gym in my apartment block," he pointed out. "A private one for the owners and their guests."

"You're not going to leave me alone now, are you?"

He smiled. "I just want to give you more pleasure."

"You just want me to marry you."

"That, too."

Holly groaned. "You're a wicked man, Richard Crawford."

"Not really," he returned. "Just a very determined one."

CHAPTER TWELVE

RICHARD sat in his office at the bank the following morning, thinking about Holly.

As determined as he was to marry her, she was just as determined to marry only for love.

Love, Richard thought scornfully. If only she knew what kind of hell love could create. He'd been in hell ever since he'd read that coroner's report.

Thinking about that reminded Richard of his thoughts after running into Kim yesterday. Maybe if he knew the truth, he might be able to find closure on the subject of Joanna once and for all.

Richard pressed the button that connected him with his PA.

Five minutes later he had what he wanted. Kim's phone number. It seemed she was still living in the Kirribilli apartment she'd lived in with her husband. No doubt it had been part of her lucrative divorce settlement.

He rang straight away, experience telling him women like Kim didn't go to work. They did charity work occasionally. Other than that, they had their hair done, went to health spas, shopped at Double Bay and lunched at Doyles. Oh, and they seduced other women's husbands.

''Hello, Kim,'' he said when she picked up on the seventh ring. Clearly not an early riser by the sound of her groggy greeting. ''It's Richard. Richard Crawford.''

''Richard! My God. Fancy you calling me. I got the impression yesterday you weren't too pleased to see me.''

''Whatever gave you that idea?'' he returned drily.

''Sarcasm, Richard?''

''I won't lie, Kim. I wasn't pleased to see you. I don't like you. I never did. Not after the way you tried to come on to me that night.''

''You really are pompous, Richard. Most men would have been flattered. But not you. You wanted to keep yourself for your one true love. Your beautiful Joanna. If only you knew the truth about your darling wife,'' she sneered down the line.

''The truth is why I'm ringing, Kim. You and Joanna were always as thick as thieves. After seeing you yesterday, I began to wonder if you knew the name of Joanna's lover, the one who fathered the child she was carrying when she died.''

''Well, well. Looks like I kept mum for nothing. You knew all along.''

''Not till after the autopsy.''

''Ri...ght. I see.''

''Was this man her first affair?''

''You want to know the absolute truth?''

Richard's hand tightened on the phone. ''That's why I'm ringing you.''

''No. It wasn't her first affair.''

Richard closed his eyes for a long moment.

''Which didn't mean that she didn't love you, Richard. She actually did, as much as Joanna could ever love anyone. She used to say you were the best she'd ever had. I guess that's why I did what I did that night. I wanted to see what she was always raving about. Joanna knew I was going to try to get you into bed. She said I wouldn't succeed and she was right.''

Richard could hardly believe what he was hearing. What kind of woman had he married?

Perhaps he would have come to realise her true nature in time. The clues had been there, he supposed, with the type of people she'd hung around. At the time, however, he'd been blinded by her beauty. And her obsessive need for him in bed. His male ego had made a fool of him.

In hindsight, however, he should have seen that her sexual greediness had reflected a greediness in her whole character, an inability to ever do without anything she'd enjoyed.

''The trouble was you weren't around enough,'' Kim flung at him almost accusingly. ''You worked such long hours. And you were always going away. She was lonely, and bored. Her job didn't involve her twenty-four seven, like yours did. She used to brag about her long lunches, most of them taken at a hotel room in town. I couldn't count the number of aspiring young writers she had a fling with.''

Richard wanted to be sick.

''But really, Richard,'' Kim raved on, ''you shouldn't feel short-changed. She was good to you, wasn't she? She was always there when you wanted her. And like I said, she loved you in her own way. Why should it worry you now if she slept around on the side? That was just sex, not love. Trust me, she wasn't having some torrid affair with the bloke who got her pregnant. She didn't even know who it was.

You were away on business and she threw this party, which developed into a bit of an orgy. She was usually very careful about using protection but things got out of hand that night. When she found out she was pregnant, she was so angry at herself. No way was she going to have a baby. She was on her way to the abortion clinic when the accident happened."

Richard had to get off that phone before he did something incredibly humiliating, like cry.

"I have to go now, Kim."

"Look, I'm sorry, Richard. But you did ask. She wasn't a bad person. Just very needy. And she did love you. Truly."

"Yeah, right. Bye, Kim."

He hung up, then just sat there, trying to make sense of it all, trying to find himself again through the wall of bitterness that had cloaked his soul for far too long.

But it was no use. He wasn't there any longer.

He stood up and walked across to the window of his office, staring down at the city below, not really seeing anything. What was the point of going on when the world was full of such wickedness?

And then he thought of Holly.

Nothing wicked about her. Even when she thought she was being wicked, she wasn't really.

If he had her in his life, he might find himself again. His spirits lifted when he thought of her being there, waiting for him, when he came home from work.

He couldn't let her run away from him. Which was what she was trying to do. She was afraid of him, because she liked being with him too much. Liked the sex too much. If only she would agree to move in with him, he could use the sex to bind her to him, to break her down and make her need him as much as he needed her.

He had to get her to move in with him. Sooner rather than later.

Whirling round, he strode over to his desk, picked up his phone and pressed Reece's number.

"Reece Diamond," Reece answered promptly.

"Reece, it's Richard. I have something I want you to do for me."

"Anything, Richard. You know that."

"I want you to act as my agent in buying a flower shop."

"A *flower* shop? That's not your usual style. Aah...I get the picture. This is for Holly, isn't it?"

"In a roundabout fashion."

"So where is this flower shop?"

"In Strathfield. It's called A Flower A Day. It's on the market with L.J. Hooker. Offer the full price they're asking, but with conditions attached to the sale."

"What conditions?"

"A very fast settlement date. This Friday."

"Can't be done that soon, mate, not if you want the books checked and proper searches done."

"I don't. Put down a substantial deposit today. I want vacant possession of the place, contracts to be exchanged this coming Friday."

"The owner might not go for that."

"If she doesn't, offer her more. Just make sure she doesn't know either your name or mine. Use my investment company name to do the deal."

"*She?* Holly owns this shop, is that it?"

"Nope. Her stepmother does."

"I don't get it."

"Holly manages the shop and lives above it."

"Now I get it," Reece said ruefully. "My God, Richard, this is not like you. You've become obsessed with this girl."

Obsessed. Yes. Obsessed just about described his condition at the moment.

"Just do what I've asked, Reece," Richard bit out. "And ring me back when they've agreed to the deal."

Reece sighed. "Okay. But be it on your head if you end up with a flower shop and no girl as well."

"I don't think that will happen."

Mondays were always slow days in the floristry industry. Holly hadn't had a customer all day. She was sitting behind her work table just after three, trying to write out a word-grabbing résumé when the doorbell tinkled.

Holly jumped to her feet just as her stepmother walked in.

Connie had always been an attractive woman. But she'd turned the clock back ten of her forty-seven years since Holly's dad had died, courtesy of a facelift done before he'd even been cold in his grave, paid for with his life insurance policy. Katie had had a few things done as well. Her big nose made smaller and her small breasts made much larger.

Holly had long been aware of the fact that Katie envied Holly her breasts. *And* her boyfriends. It was no surprise, in hindsight, that Katie had stolen Dave. Though Holly suspected it wasn't Katie's new big boobs that Dave wanted so much, but her source of money. Connie had never been able to deny her daughter anything she wanted. She was already talking about a big, fancy wedding.

Holly could only hope that, some day, some fortune-hunting man would come along and con Connie, as she'd conned Holly's Dad. The woman had never loved him. Holly could see that now as well.

Holly looked at her stepmother with genuine distaste as the woman walked towards her with a plastic smile on her plastic face. Even her blonde hair looked plastic.

"Hello, Holly," Connie said breezily. "I have some wonderful news."

"Really?" She couldn't imagine what.

"The shop was sold today, and I didn't have to drop the price I was asking at all."

Holly's heart started thudding. "But...but...nobody's even been in here to inspect it. Or looked at the books!"

"The buyer probably isn't interested in it as a flower shop. I dare say he just wants the property. He also wants a quick settlement. Contracts will be exchanged this Friday. Unfortunately, you have to be out of here by then. It's a vacant possession deal."

Holly felt as if someone had just punched her in the stomach. She'd thought it would be ages before the shop sold. Months and months.

"But you don't have to worry, dear," Connie continued in a sickly sweet, pseudo-conciliatory tone. "I've signed a cheque for you for ten thousand dollars. Here it is." And she placed the slip of paper on the table Holly was now holding onto for dear life.

"That should be more than enough for you to live on while you find another place and another job. Which won't present a problem, I'm sure, since you're such an excellent florist."

Holly picked up the cheque, staring down at it before glancing up at her stepmother.

"You think this is enough to compensate for all the work I've put into this business?" she ground out. "I've worked six days a week since Dad died. I've taken a pittance of a salary and done the books as well. I deserve half the business, Connie. You know that."

Connie drew herself up straight, her tautly unlined face growing haughty at the same time. "I know no such thing. You've been paid quite adequately. After all, you've had a free flat to live in. Not to mention unlimited use of the delivery van. Free flowers as well!"

Free *flowers*! That did it. That absolutely did it!

"If you don't give me what's due to me, Connie, I'll take you to court."

Connie laughed. "Do that and you'll end up with nothing. Or less than nothing, once you've paid your lawyer and court costs. I was married to your father for eight years, missie. Judges are very sympathetic to widows, not vindictive young daughters who have the means to make their own way in life. For pity's sake, Holly," she spat, "don't be a fool!"

"I am not a fool. You're the fool if you think I'm going to let you sell my dad's business and give me nothing. You're a greedy bitch. You never loved my dad. You only married him for what you could get out of him."

"I held up my part of the bargain. Your dad wanted a sexy, good-looking wife. Well, he got one. It wasn't easy going to bed with a man I wasn't attracted to, but I did. I earned every cent I got from him and I aim to keep every cent, so don't you threaten me, Holly Greenaway. I'm a lot tougher than the likes of you. If you take me to court I'll have Katie up on the witness stand telling the judge how much of your dad's money you wasted on clothes and boys and drugs and God knows what. You want to play dirty, girl, then just watch me!"

Holly gaped at the woman. My God, she was more than a mercenary bitch. She was evil.

Connie's face turned ugly as it twisted into a sneer. "I suggest you take that money and run, because that's all you're going to get!"

Holly looked the woman straight in the eye as she tore the cheque into little pieces. "You think so? I'm going to get my dad's shop," she said with a bitter resolve. "*All* of it. And I won't even have to take you to court. Just you wait and see."

"In your dreams, girlie. Katie always said you were a dreamer. Be out of this place by Friday morning, or I'll have you thrown out." Spinning on her heels, Connie stormed out without a backward glance.

When Holly felt tears begin to threaten, she forced them back. No tears. Not this time. This time she was going to do what Mrs Crawford said a woman had to do sometimes.

Act like a man!

Flipping over her phone and address book, she memorised the number she'd entered under C just that morning, and which Richard had given her yesterday.

"Ring me any time," he'd said.

Her hand only shook a little as she picked up her phone, then punched his number in.

"Richard," she said when he answered. "It's Holly. I...I need to see you." Darn, but that didn't sound at all as a man would sound.

"Now," she added swiftly. "I need to see you *now*!"

Much better.

"My God, Holly, what's wrong? What's happened, my darling?"

Oh, dear. He shouldn't have called her his darling.

"I...I..."

"Yes?"

She tried again. "The thing is, Richard..."

"Yes?"

No use. She burst into tears.

Richard gripped the steering wheel of his BMW as he threaded his way through the city traffic, heading for Strathfield, and Holly.

"Damn and blast," he swore when he struck another set of red lights.

But it wasn't the driving delays that were distressing him the most, but his own disgusting self. What had possessed him to think he could play with a person's life as he had just played with Holly's?

There was no excuse. Buying the flower shop and having her chucked out, just so she would run to him, was the behaviour of an out-and-out bastard. When she'd broken down on the phone and sobbed out her confrontation with her stepmother, Richard had wanted to cut his own throat.

Holly's pain had been palpable, even over the phone.

Richard could not believe how insensitive he'd been to do something like that.

At the same time, he could not deny that there was a part of him that felt satisfaction. She had turned to him. Straight away. Without any hesitation.

No matter how cruel his strategy had been, it had worked.

For the rest of the drive to Strathfield, he tried convincing himself that the end justified the means. He would be good to her. Very good. He'd help her move, help her find a new job. He might even buy her another shop, if she'd let him. A better shop. Her life would be better, with him.

She'd stopped crying by the time he arrived, her face surprisingly composed as he hurried in through the door.

"I'm glad you came," she said, in a very odd voice for a girl who'd been beside herself less than half an hour earlier.

Richard slowed his step.

"I had planned to talk to you about this on the phone," she went on, again in that strangely cool voice. "But it didn't work out that way. We dreamers take a while to get our heads out of the clouds and into the real world."

Now she sounded bitter. And terribly hard!

"Anyway, I have a proposition for you."

Richard ground to a halt. "A proposition?"

"Yes. Do you still want to marry me?"

He blinked. Crikey!

"Of course," he said immediately.

''Buy me this shop and I'll marry you.''

Buy her this shop. Hell, he already owned the damned thing.

''The contracts haven't been exchanged yet,'' she went on. ''All you have to do is contact the real estate agency and gazump the bid. My stepmother will drop that other buyer like a hotcake. Contracts haven't been signed so it's still up for grabs.''

Richard could not believe things had turned out this well.

And yet...

''You said you wouldn't marry for any reason other than love,'' he threw at her.

Her eyes softened, reminding him of the warm, loving, sensual girl he'd spent the weekend with. But then, suddenly, they hardened again.

''Don't argue with me, Richard. Will you do this for me, or not?''

''I'll do it today.''

She breathed in deeply, then let it out in one long, shuddering sigh. ''Good. One other thing.''

''Yes?''

''Take me away somewhere. I...I have to get away from here for a while.''

He saw it then, the fragility behind the superficial hardness. She was like a thin sheet of glass. One little shake and she would shatter. Getting her right away would be a good idea. He wouldn't mind a break himself.

''Where would you like to go?'' he asked gently.

''I don't care,'' she said, desperation in her eyes. ''Anywhere, as long as it's a long way from here.''

''Do you have a current passport?''

"Of course not," she said with a bitter laugh. "You're looking at a go-nowhere nobody. A fool and a dreamer."

"I don't think you're a fool," he said, making his way slowly towards her. "And I don't think there's anything wrong with being a dreamer, as long as you dream nice dreams."

"I dreamt of owning Dad's flower shop," she said, her voice breaking off with a sob.

"I know, darling," he said softly, and gathered her into his arms. "I know."

"Oh, Richard," she cried, and buried her face in his chest, her hands clutching at the lapels of his suit jacket. "She was so horrid. So hateful! I don't understand people like that."

"Don't think about her any more, Holly. Put her out of your mind and out of your life. People like that are poison. And don't worry. This shop will be all yours by the end of the day. I promise."

"And I'll be all yours," she returned on a whisper, then began to cry again.

Richard tightened his hold on her, telling himself that he was doing the right thing. But he knew he wasn't.

She'd once said how corrupting it must be to be able to buy anything you wanted. It seemed it was. He'd wanted Holly as his bride. And he was about to buy her, even though he knew it was wrong.

"I'm sorry, but I'm going to have to love you and leave you, Holly," he said, putting her at arm's length. "I have to get onto the real estate agent before they shut up shop today. I suggest you get busy as well. You said you have a girl who comes in sometimes to help you?''

''Yes, Sara. She comes from Wednesday till Saturday.''

''Would she look after the shop for you if you went away tomorrow?''

''I'm sure she would. Did you say *tomorrow*?''

''Yes, I'm going to see if I can get tickets on the *Spirit of Tasmania.* I know it leaves Sydney for Tasmania every Tuesday afternoon.''

''Tasmania!'' Her lovely eyes lit up. ''Oh, I've always wanted to go there. I saw a segment on a holiday programme on TV about that trip. You can take your car on the ferry and they have proper cabins and everything. It'll be like a mini cruise.''

''I'm glad you like the idea.'' Richard was struck with a momentary crisis of conscience. ''Are you absolutely sure you want to do this, Holly? The shop, and the marriage, and everything.''

Her eyes cleared. Her chin lifted. ''Absolutely.''

''So be it,'' he said.

CHAPTER THIRTEEN

"LOOK, Richard!" Holly exclaimed. "We're going under the Harbour Bridge! Doesn't it look fabulous from down here?"

"It sure does," he agreed.

They were standing out on the back deck of the *Spirit Of Tasmania*, along with several other passengers, enjoying the warmth of the afternoon sunshine and the wonderful sights of the city as the ferry made its way slowly from the wharf at Darling Harbour towards Sydney Heads.

"I still can't believe how quickly you did everything," Holly said, with an awed glance up at the handsome man next to her. "The shop. This trip. My ring..." She looked back down at her left hand, and the glorious diamond engagement ring sparkling on her ring finger.

"My mother says I'm an overachiever."

Holly smiled up at him. "In that case, I *like* overachievers." She would have preferred to say love. But overnight, Holly had come to terms with her one-sided love for Richard. He did care about her. And he was totally committed to their marriage. That meant a lot. And who knew? In time, the memory of his wife would surely fade. Joanna was dead and Holly was here, in the flesh, to look after him, and love him.

Miracles did happen. After all, who would have

believed she'd shortly be the proud owner of A Flower A Day? Or living in that incredible penthouse? Or having a man like Richard as her husband and the father of her children?

On the other hand, there was no getting round the fact that her impulsive decision to let Richard buy her as his wife was no miracle. It had been partly inspired by fury. A fury that hadn't yet abated.

"By the way, Richard," she said. "I want Connie to know that the shop was bought for me by my fiancé. Can you arrange that?" She liked imagining the looks on Katie's and Dave's faces as well, when they heard the news. She hoped they all choked on it.

"Of course," Richard returned. "But best leave such a surprise till after the contracts are exchanged, don't you think?"

"Yes, you're right. That bitch might pull out of the sale, if she thinks I'm going to get the shop. You *are* a wise man."

Wise, and wonderfully passionate. Holly could forgive Richard for not loving her, if his passion for her remained intact. Last night he'd been especially passionate.

A sudden thought occurred to her. Oh, dear, oh, dear. How could she have been so stupid?

"Richard," she whispered urgently.

"What?" he whispered back, bending his head down sidewards.

"In all the hurry to pack, I...um...I forgot to bring my pills."

"Is that such a problem? I mean, we both want children, Holly. And I, for one, don't want to wait too long. Why not just forget the pill from now on?"

"No, you don't understand. I'm happy to have your

baby. But first, I'm sure to get a period in a day or two. And the thing is…I don't like…I mean…''

''I understand, Holly. Truly.''

''Are you sure?''

''Please don't stress, darling. I'm not here with you just for sex. Besides, we still have tonight. Though I'll probably have a bad back in the morning if I attempt too much in that teensy-weensy cabin of ours with its teensy-weensy bunks and teensy-weensy shower.''

''They certainly didn't choose those beds with a man like you in mind,'' Holly agreed, relieved that Richard wasn't annoyed with her.

''I'll manage,'' he said. ''I noticed a nice firm little table between the bunks, and another one under the mirror. Not as good as my desk, or your work table in the shop last night, but necessity is the mother of invention.''

''Shh,'' she warned, glancing over at the elderly couple standing next to them.

''You're right,'' Richard murmured. ''Wouldn't want our fellow passengers to hear too much about our X-rated love life. The shock might do them in.''

Holly knew what Richard meant. Most of the people on the ferry were on the older side. Retired couples going to Tasmania on holiday together. She supposed it was a good way to travel, taking their own cars with them. But she wondered if some might have been better on bus tours, especially the ones using walking sticks!

''Do you think we'll still be going away on holidays together when we're their age?'' she said a bit wistfully.

''Absolutely,'' he replied.

"We'll have to keep fit."

"We'll keep fit running after our children. Look, the Heads are coming up," Richard said, pointing towards the impressive promontories that guarded the entrance to Port Jackson. "It's calm here in the harbour but things might get a bit rougher once we're out to sea. Do you get seasick?"

"I don't know."

"You'd better come with me, then. I brought some tablets, just in case."

Typical of Richard, she thought as he took her arm and led her inside off the deck. He was a planner, as well as a doer. She would always feel safe with him at her side.

Making their way back to the cabin took a few minutes. The cabins were located on a different level at the front of the boat, with lots of narrow hallways going every which way, rather like a rabbit warren.

Still, Richard seemed to know where they were going.

"No, it's this way," he said when she went to turn in the wrong direction at the end of a long corridor.

Holly realised she was going to learn a lot about her husband-to-be during the ten days they would be away. Their return ticket was for Thursday week, docking back at Darling Harbour on the Friday.

"You know your mother told me recently that the best way for two people to find out if they can get along is to go away together."

"In that case, we're doing exceptionally well so far. Already an hour on the boat and we haven't argued once."

"You're obviously on your best behaviour. But can you keep it up?"

''It'll be a challenge,'' he said with a devilish twinkle in his eye. ''But I'll do my best.''

Holly punched him on one of his rock-hard biceps. ''Your mother didn't tell me you were so bad. She always said you were such a good boy.''

''Never believe anything mothers say about their sons,'' he said as they reached their cabin. ''But speaking of my mother,'' he added once they were inside, ''I got an email from her this morning. Clever Melvin took a laptop with him and gave me his email address. So I sent them an announcement of our engagement.''

''Oh, Richard, you didn't!'' Holly had assumed he'd keep that a secret for a while. ''I hope you didn't tell her about the shop business. I *like* your mother, Richard. And she likes me. The last thing I want is for her to start thinking I'm some kind of fortune hunter!''

''Trust me, she doesn't. I *did* tell her I'd bought the shop for you and she was very happy about it. I also told her that I was crazy about you and that I was taking you away to Tassie for a well-needed break. I also informed her that we were getting married as soon as she got back.''

Holly blinked. ''And…and what did she say?'' Holly couldn't help wondering how Mrs Crawford interpreted Richard saying he was crazy about her. Did she think that meant he'd fallen in love with her; that he was finally over Joanna's death?

Holly supposed it didn't matter if the woman thought that. Other people would. To be honest, Holly preferred that they did. She didn't want people thinking their marriage was like Reece and Alanna's.

"Mum was tickled pink. She said we might have a double wedding."

"She and Melvin?"

"Yep. He popped the question and she said yes."

"That's wonderful!"

"Yes, they're well suited, that pair. Just like us."

Holly could see that she and Richard *were* quite well suited. But he *was* twelve years older than she was. Older and much more experienced. She wondered if he was like a father-figure to her. If that was his main attraction for her.

"You're thinking again," Richard said. "I hate it when you do that. I never know quite *what* you're thinking."

"Don't you?" That surprised her. She imagined he'd always read her every thought and move. "You mean I'm a woman of mystery?"

"Irritatingly so at times."

"What am I thinking now?" she said, her eyes raking down over his body.

"Now *that*, I can read," he growled.

"Be careful now," she said laughingly when he pulled her down onto the narrow bed with him.

"Why don't you shut up, woman?" And he kissed her.

It was a good hour later before Holly got round to taking the seasickness tablet.

"What would you like to do now?" Richard asked after they'd both straightened their clothes and combed their hair.

"We could pop along and check out that café we came past," she suggested. "Or, even better, we could go along to the bar and have a drink? We don't have to drive anywhere."

"*We?*" he said, his eyes narrowing on her as he moved very close.

The smallness of the cabin plus his looming over her by some inches reminded Holly of what a big man Richard was. He was intimidating in size, as well as in manner.

But she wasn't afraid of him any more. Not one little bit.

"You don't think I'm going to let you do all the driving during this trip, do you?" she tossed up at him saucily.

"Hmm. Perhaps we should get one thing straight, madam. I like to do the driving in my own car."

"Is that so?" she returned, arms crossing. "Methinks we're just about to have our first argument."

"No, no," he said, lifting up his hands in swift surrender. "No arguing. You can drive. Sometimes. If you're extra careful."

"Typical male."

"Yes," he agreed. "I'm a typical male. Sorry about that. But when we get back to Sydney I'll buy you your own car. What would you like?"

Holly was taken aback. Just like that. A new car. One part of her thrilled to the idea of driving round in her own new car. But there was another part of her that worried Richard was buying her again.

Silly, really. They were going to be husband and wife. Why shouldn't he buy her a new car? But as much as she tried to be logical about it, she still didn't like it.

"I...I don't know," she said. "I'll think about it."

CHAPTER FOURTEEN

SUNDAY saw them driving into Hobart, Tasmania's capital city. Situated on the estuary of the Derwent River, on the lower east side of the island, Hobart was one of Australia's oldest and most beautiful cities.

"Reminds me of some of the large port towns in the south of England," Richard said as they drove slowly along the harbour foreshore, which was only a stone's throw from the CBD.

"I've never been overseas, so I wouldn't know," Holly said. "All I can say is that it's very picturesque, with almost as good a harbour as Sydney."

There were lots of boats of all shapes and sizes moored against the many piers, from small runabouts to expensive-looking speedboats and racing yachts. In the distance, a massive, grey-painted catamaran was churning across the wide expanse of water, looking quite magnificent, but rather menacing. Richard speculated that it had to belong to the armed forces.

"Could even be American," he said.

Further along, a white ocean liner was anchored against a jetty, glistening in the sunshine. It made the ferry they'd travelled down on look small, yet Holly had thought the *Spirit of Tasmania* very large when she'd first seen it docked at Darling Harbour.

"Did you know Hobart has the second deepest harbour in the world?'' Richard said when she commented on the size of the liner.

''What's the deepest?'' she asked, curious.

''Rio.''

''How do you know such things?''

He shrugged. ''I read a lot. I also have a photographic memory. Made studying for exams a lot easier, I can tell you.''

''I never had to sit for any proper exams,'' Holly said without thinking. ''I never even sat for my school certificate. I left school at fifteen to work with Dad in the shop.'' That feeling of inferiority flooded Holly with her admissions. ''You must think me very ignorant.''

''I don't think you're at all ignorant. Just the opposite. I think you're a very smart girl. Look at the way you did those books without any formal training. Passing exams is no gauge to a person's intelligence, Holly. Simply their ability to recall facts and figures.''

''You might think that way, but a lot of people don't. They think a degree is the be-all and end-all.''

''It isn't.''

''That's easy for you to say. You have your degree. It's a bit like people saying money isn't important when they already have it. Try not having any money and see how important it suddenly becomes.''

Holly had no idea how she got onto this subject. But she regretted it immediately. Regretted her sharp tone as well.

The past few days had been so wonderful. The first night of their trip—the night before she'd got her period—they'd stayed at this lovely historical house. It had originally been a doctor's residence before it had become a hospital during the late nineteenth century. Now, it was a B & B.

The owner had taken them for a tour when they'd arrived, telling them its history and showing them all the rooms with their many antiques, pointing out that the spacious suite they were sleeping in had been where the babies were born.

It had been decorated in blue with a big brass bed and a wonderfully romantic atmosphere.

That night, Richard had made love to her in the big brass bed for ages. Really made love to her. Very tenderly, telling her all the while that soon *they'd* be making a baby. The next morning, when she'd looked at him over breakfast Holly had felt more confident than ever that their marriage would work.

They'd driven across the north-eastern part of Tasmania on the Thursday and Friday, exploring the countryside by day, and relaxing over a fine meal each night, discovering that they didn't need to be having sex to enjoy each other's company. They'd stayed at a different place every night, another historic home that had been converted to a boutique hotel on the Thursday, a B & B in Swansea on Friday and a guest-house in Richmond last night.

Holly had never realised till she came here just how beautiful and interesting Tasmania was. Very rich in history. Richard thought the same. Every night, both of them had devoured the travel brochures they'd picked up on the ferry, seeing where they could go and what they could do the next day. Next Tuesday they planned to drive down to Port Arthur, the famous old convict jail, after which they would follow the highway up the east coast before crossing to Devonport for the ferry's departure on Thursday.

Holly had been very excited about their plans. So why had she risked spoiling everything with such provocative comments? She might not be ignorant, but she was a complete idiot!

"I'm sorry, Richard," she said swiftly. "I wish I hadn't said any of that. It sounded petty. And bitter. I'm a bit touchy about education. Connie used to lord it over Dad that she had some fancy arts degree. Katie went to university as well, and of course Dad paid for it all."

"I can well understand why you would feel resentful, Holly," he said. "Don't apologise for your feelings. You're a human being, not a saint. But higher education can be highly overrated. As far as money is concerned, everyone likes having money and I'm no exception. I've worked very hard accumulating lots of it and I enjoy the power it gives me. It *is* satisfying to be able to buy just about anything you want. I won't deny that, either. You wouldn't be sitting here with me now if it wasn't for my money."

"Don't say that!"

"Why not? It's true."

Clearly, from his point of view, however, he *had* bought her. Lock, stock, and barrel.

"There were other considerations," she felt forced to say. "I would not have made my proposition in the first place if I hadn't liked you as much as I do."

"And if the sex wasn't as good," Richard added with a dry laugh, even whilst his heart twisted.

It was his own silly fault, of course. He'd set out to bind her to him through sex.

He seemed to have succeeded all too well.

How perverse it was to find that he now resented Holly liking his lovemaking as much as she obviously did. No doubt the reason for her stroppiness this morning was frustration. Three whole days without an orgasm! Underneath, she was probably panting for him to take her straight to the hotel, and to bed.

The thought both repelled and excited him.

''You said it would be all systems clear for a resumption of relations today, didn't you?'' he asked with a long sidewards glance, noting the instant pink in her cheeks.

Yet it was very cool in the car, the air-conditioning doing a good job of keeping the heat out. Outside, the temperature was thirty degrees, the sun very bright.

''Yes,'' she said tautly.

''Just as well we're not far from the hotel then,'' he muttered, his own body already stirring.

Richard had chosen the Wrest Point Casino to stay in, not because of the gambling facilities, but because it was one of Hobart's top hotels. Situated on a point overlooking the water, the circular tower building boasted five-star rooms, all with magnificent views of the river, which was as wide as it was deep.

A circular driveway led up to the entrance of the hotel, a smartly dressed parking valet jumping to attention as soon as Richard stopped. The reception staff was just as efficient, and they were soon riding the lift up to their allotted floor. Their luggage was just being delivered as they reached the door, Richard giving the young man a tip, even though he didn't have to. Australia was not large on tipping, but Richard had found it was never a bad idea.

Money did smooth one's path in life, he thought ruefully as he ushered Holly into their five-star room. It bought you the best of accommodation, and the most accommodating of women.

Despite his throbbing erection and Holly's admission that his lovemaking was one of the reasons she was here, Richard resisted the temptation to pull her into his arms as soon as the porter departed. Instead, he strolled across to the window, pretending that he found the magnificent water view much more interesting than Holly.

When he slowly turned, he found her standing there in the middle of the spacious room, looking slightly confused, and incredibly sexy.

Not that she was dressed sexily. Her white shorts were a modest length and her simple pink blouse didn't cling. Her long tanned legs were bare, however, and her hair was down, the way he liked it. Her make-up was zilch, other than a touch of red lipstick.

"Are you angry with me for some reason?" she asked at last.

"Not at all," he lied.

"Then why are you acting like this?"

"Like what?"

"Like you don't want to make love to me."

"You want me to make love to you?" he said, hating himself for being such an idiot.

"I thought that was what you wanted, too."

"I need to have a shower first. We've been travelling all day and I feel hot and sticky. Of course, you're welcome to join me, if you like..."

Let *her* make love to *him*, if that was what she wanted so much. With her hands and her mouth.

She stared at him the way she'd stared at him the first day he'd met her, her eyes totally inscrutable. If only he knew what she was thinking…

Her smile blew him away.

"You know I like," she said, her eyes going all soft and smoky.

Richard had often read about women going weak at the knees with desire. He'd never imagined being afflicted in a similar manner. He leant back against the wall and gripped the window-sill.

"You'll have to be gentle with me," he drawled, hoping to hide his unexpected vulnerability with humour. "All that driving has made me exhausted."

"Poor Richard," she purred. "Perhaps a bath would be a better idea. I'll go and run one for you." And she was gone.

Richard closed his eyes at the sound of the water running.

A bath. With her, naked. Her, washing him. All over. Her, kissing him and caressing him in the water.

His knuckles whitened on the sill as he envisaged what would happen after that. He'd have her dry him but leave herself wet. Then he'd carry her to bed where he'd lick her dry. All over. He'd make her cry out under his mouth. Then cry out under him.

He wanted her to lose herself entirely. Lose control. He needed to see that she was totally his. At least in bed.

"Are you coming?"

His eyes opened, his breath catching to find her

standing in the doorway of the bathroom, already naked.

He'd never seen her look more beautiful, or more desirable.

''Absolutely,'' he said, laughing with dark humour as he propelled himself towards her.

CHAPTER FIFTEEN

"I SHOULD never have let you buy me all those clothes," Holly muttered over the rim of her coffee-cup.

Richard glanced up from his cappuccino in surprise. It was Monday, and they were sitting together in a cosy little coffee shop in Sandy Bay, the Hobart suburb that boasted the casino and lots of trendy boutiques. Richard had thoroughly enjoyed himself all morning, taking her to the most expensive dress shops, having her try on outfits for him, choosing only the best to buy. He'd got over his irrational burst of resentment yesterday, telling himself not to be such a fool. It was great that she liked him making love to her, that she wasn't at all inhibited, or prudish.

"What on earth are you talking about?" he demanded to know. "Why shouldn't I have bought you those clothes? They're classy clothes, nothing like that dress Reece bought Alanna."

She shook her head, her eyes worrying him. "I'm sorry, Richard."

"Sorry? What do you mean you're sorry? Sorry about what?"

Her coffee-cup clattered back into its saucer. "I can't marry you. I thought I could, but I can't."

Richard tried not to panic.

"Why?" he grated out.

"It simply won't work," she said.

"Why won't it work?"

"You know why. I told you once. I need my husband to love me. *Me*, Holly Greenaway. I'm a living, breathing person, Richard, not a possession. You made me feel like a possession this morning. Like a trophy wife, to be made over into what you want. When we go back to the hotel after this and you...you want me to do the kind of things you like, I'll feel I *have* to, not because I *want* to. Those clothes feel like payment for services rendered, as well as services yet to be rendered. Same with the new car you offered me. Same with the shop, too."

"The shop was your idea," he bit out, an emotional storm building up inside him. "So was the marriage proposal."

"Yes. Yes, you're right. I let your wealth corrupt me into getting what *I* wanted. That, and your skill in bed. But it has to stop now, before I get pregnant. I'm sorry about the shop. But you won't lose by buying it. I'm sure it will be a good long-term investment. All I ask is for you to let me stay on there till I can find another job and another place to live." She wiggled the engagement ring off her finger and placed it in the middle of the table.

He could not believe it. She was rejecting him. Running out on him.

The need to strike out at her, to hurt her as he was hurting, was intense.

"I'll be selling that bloody shop," he growled. "I should never have bought it in the first place. Which I did, you know. There never was any other buyer. It was me all along."

She stared at him, and for the first time Richard

had no doubt about what he was seeing in her eyes. Total shock. And then, the most dreadful dismay.

''Oh, Richard,'' she said brokenly. ''How could you? I always thought you were a man of honour.''

''Nice men finish last, sweetheart,'' he threw at her, talking tough, but inside he was disintegrating.

A sob broke from her throat. ''Oh, God. I have to get out of here.''

She jumped up, her chair falling back. She almost tripped over the bags at her feet as she fled. Richard hesitated only a moment before he was up and after her, leaving everything behind. The ring. The clothes. None of them mattered. All that mattered was Holly. He had to get her and tell her how sorry he was. He would try to explain and beg her to forgive him.

''Holly!'' he called after her as he pushed through the coffee-shop door in her wake.

She halted at the kerb just long enough to send a distressed glance over her shoulder at him. Then she dashed out into the road.

The loud screech of brakes assaulted Richard's ears as he saw a white van hurtling down the hill towards her.

They said your life flashed before you the moment before you died. The *truth* flashed before Richard's eyes the moment before he thought Holly would die.

He loved her. Loved her as he'd never loved Joanna.

The thought of burying Holly gave him a strength and a speed that was inhuman. Some guardian angel must have lifted him and propelled him across that road, because before he knew it he was diving into mid-air, taking her with him out of harm's way.

She screamed as they crashed into the gutter on the other side, Richard's body buffering hers against the fall. Richard didn't scream. He was thanking God for his mercy.

People quickly milled around them, helping them to their feet, asking if they were all right. The driver from the white van, which had stopped. People from the coffee shop. Passers-by.

''I...I think so,'' Holly said shakily. ''Richard? Are you all right?''

''I'm fine,'' he insisted, even as his leg throbbed with pain under his trousers. Thank God the weather had turned cool that day and he'd been wearing a leather jacket, or all his arms would have been grazed.

''Your face is bleeding,'' Holly said, reaching up to touch his cheek.

Someone produced some tissues, which he dabbed against his cut cheekbone.

''Come back into the coffee shop,'' the lady proprietor insisted. ''You've had a bad shock. A sit down and a hot sweet drink is called for.''

Holly knew the woman was right. She also knew Richard had just saved her life. But to go back and sit down with him. To have to *talk* to him.

''Please, Holly,'' he said, perhaps guessing that she still wanted to flee.

She closed her eyes rather than look at him. He took her arm and led her back across the road to the coffee shop. She finally opened her eyes after she'd been settled back in the chair she'd occupied earlier. The sight of her engagement ring still in the middle of the table brought back the reasons for her fleeing in the first place.

Richard's admission to buying the shop behind her back.

Why? The reason was obvious. He'd wanted her to be evicted. Wanted her to have nowhere else to go, but him.

Two new cups of milk coffee arrived, into which the waitress heaped some sugar.

"Drink up, dears," she advised before leaving them to it.

Holly just sat there, saying nothing.

"You shouldn't have run like that, Holly," Richard said quietly at last. "You could have been killed."

"Better dead than wed to a man like you."

"Don't say that," he choked out, his face ashen. "I love you, Holly. I know you won't believe me, but it's true."

"How dare you?" she snapped under her breath. "It's despicable to lie about something like that! But then you *are* despicable."

"I couldn't agree with you more. What I did was despicable. But I do love you."

"You simply can't accept defeat, can you? You don't love me," she said bitterly. "Everyone knows you're still in love with Joanna. Your mother. Your friends. I'm just a means to an end."

"That's not true."

"Don't you dare try to tell me what's true and what isn't. I *know* the truth."

"No, you don't," he bit out. "And neither does anyone else. You think I'm still in love with Joanna? Well, you're wrong. I hate her. No, that's wrong. I don't even hate her any more. She's not worthy of being hated. Because that would mean she was worthy of being loved.''

Holly gaped at him.

''Yes, well you might be surprised. But I couldn't let anyone know I was married to an unfaithful bitch, could I? Not me. Mr Successful. Impossible to tell anyone that she'd been expecting a child when she was killed, especially when that child definitely wasn't mine. Ever since she died I thought she'd been having an affair and that she'd been going to pass the child off as mine. But Kim finally filled in the gaps for me when I rang her the other day and demanded to know the truth. Joanna was going to have an abortion on the day she was killed. She didn't even *know* who the father of her child was. It could have been any of half a dozen men she let screw her at a party she threw when I was away. Isn't that a lovely thought? My wife, a slut!''

Holly could not think of a thing to say as shock warred with sympathy for Richard. How dreadful to discover that the person you loved was so…sick. She'd been shattered when Dave had dumped her for Katie. What if she'd been married to Dave and discovered he'd been sleeping around like a tom-cat and had made some other girl pregnant?

''Oh, Richard,'' she said at last, feeling truly sorry for him.

Holly was appalled when tears glistened in his eyes.

''Don't cry, Richard,'' she pleaded. ''Please don't cry.''

''I'm not crying for her, Holly. Let the devil take her. I'm sure he has. But I feel like crying over losing you,'' he choked out. ''You have no idea how much I love you.''

''Do you, Richard? Do you, really?''

''More than words can say. You brought me back from the edge of darkness. You gave me hope for a future. You showed me that love doesn't have to be selfish.''

''Then why did you buy the shop?''

He shook his head. ''It was a mistake. I'd just found out from Kim how truly wicked Joanna was and I was afraid for my sanity. I needed you, Holly. Needed your warmth and your kindness. And, yes, the comfort of your body. I was too blind with bitterness to see that my feelings for you had already deepened to love. It wasn't till I saw that car coming towards you a little while ago that the truth hit me. I do realise that you will still find it hard to forgive me. But give me another chance, Holly. You must feel something for me. Maybe, one day, you might learn to love me.''

''I don't think so, Richard,'' she said quietly. When she picked up the ring and slipped it back onto her finger, his head snapped back with shock.

Her smile was soft and loving. ''You see, I've been in love with you for quite a while, my darling,'' she said, reaching over to take one of his hands in hers.

His eyes filled with tears again, and this time she wasn't appalled. There was something about a man who could cry over her that was very lovable indeed.

CHAPTER SIXTEEN

"THANK you so much for giving me away, Melvin," Holly said sincerely.

"My pleasure, sweetie," Melvin replied.

Holly thought *he* was the sweetie. He was such a nice man. So kind and considerate. Melvin and Mrs Crawford had surprised everyone by tying the knot whilst they were overseas. But they'd been home for a few weeks now and Holly had never known a happier couple.

Not counting herself and Richard, of course, she amended with a sigh. They were so happy together, even more so since she'd found out last month that she was expecting a baby. Already, Richard had given Reece the job of finding them the right family home. No way, he said, was he going to raise a child of his in a penthouse.

"Not nervous, are you?" Melvin whispered as he took her arm.

"Just a little," Holly returned. The day so far had been somewhat nerve-racking, trying to get everything right, making sure she looked as good as she could possibly look.

"No reason to be," he said, and patted her arm. "You look divine. And you're marrying a fine man."

Holly had no doubts about that. But she still felt a bit jittery as she glanced up the aisle.

Her eyes landed first on Alanna and Sara, who were slowly making their way towards the front of the church, both of them looking extremely svelte and elegant in red. Their long satin dresses were the same colour as the bouquet of red roses Holly was holding, a sentimental choice because of the way she and Richard had met.

Her bridesmaids' bouquets, however, were of white roses, matching Holly's dazzlingly white gown. She hadn't wanted to wear cream or ivory. Her satin gown was also not straight, like theirs, but had a traditionally large skirt, gathered out from a tightly boned bodice that showed her hourglass figure. The neckline was wide and low, the sleeves long and tight. Her tulle veil stretched out into a train, seeded with small pearls around the edges.

Alanna and Sara had said she looked like a princess. But what they thought didn't really matter. All Holly really cared about was what Richard thought of her.

Her agitated gaze finally reached the three men standing up near the priest who was to conduct the ceremony.

Each one of them looked very handsome in their black dinner suits, even Mike, who'd scrubbed up remarkably well after a shave and a haircut. He really was an unusual man. Very intense, with a darkly brooding nature, which could be interesting, if you liked that kind of thing.

Fortunately Sara, who was partnering him today, wasn't one of those women who'd taken an instant fancy to him. Her husband wouldn't have been too pleased if she had.

Reece, of course, looked as glamorous as usual. He and Alanna would always be a striking couple. Holly had finally warmed to Reece, and she *really* liked Alanna, who'd taken her under her wing and been such a help with all the wedding preparations, which had been considerable.

Finally, Holly allowed her eyes to move over to Richard, who was looking absolutely gorgeous but just a little nervous too, she thought with a relieved smile.

No one else would have noticed. They would just see a tall, handsome man with steely grey eyes and a dignified expression.

But Holly knew him better than anyone by now. His hands were clasped just a little too tightly together down in front of him for true composure. And his lips were pressed into a firm line as well.

She liked it that he loved her so much that he would be nervous on his wedding day. Richard was not a man who ever showed nerves.

Holly suspected she would never see him cry again, as he had that day in Tasmania. But the memory of that day would always stay with her. Thinking of it right now reassured her.

Richard loved her. Truly loved her. Her, Holly Greenaway.

You would have liked him, Dad, she whispered in her mind as she walked up the aisle to marry the man she loved.

Mrs Crawford beamed at her from where she was

sitting in the front pew, looking amazingly young in lemon silk.

They hadn't told her about the baby yet, but she was going to be thrilled when she found out. But not as thrilled as Holly.

She was going to have a baby. She and Richard were going to be a family. Holly's heart turned over with happiness. She hadn't been part of a family for so long.

Finally, Alanna moved away from the aisle to the side and Richard had a clearer view of his bride.

He sucked in sharply.

''I admit I was wrong, Rich,'' Reece murmured by his side. ''She's definitely the girl for you.''

''Too young for him, I reckon,'' Mike muttered, and Reece jabbed him in the ribs.

Mike grunted. ''Okay, okay, she does love him. I can see that. Even worse, I think he loves her.''

''What's wrong with that?'' Reece said sharply.

''Hush up, you two,'' Richard commanded. ''I'm getting married here.''

Really married this time, he thought as his lovely Holly reached his side. This is the real thing. This is *real* love.

His heart squeezed tight as he reached out his hand to her. She smiled as she took it, a warm, loving smile that made him relax for the first time that day.

''You look incredible,'' he whispered, still in awe of her. ''Exquisite.''

''Thank you,'' she whispered back.

I should be thanking you, my darling, he thought

as they turned to face the priest together. For loving me. And forgiving me. And trusting me again.

I won't ever let you down, he promised her silently as the priest started talking about the sacredness of marriage. I will protect you with my life. And I will love you to my dying day…

If you enjoyed what you just read,
then we've got an offer you can't resist!
Take 2 bestselling
love stories FREE!
Plus get a FREE surprise gift!

Coming Next Month

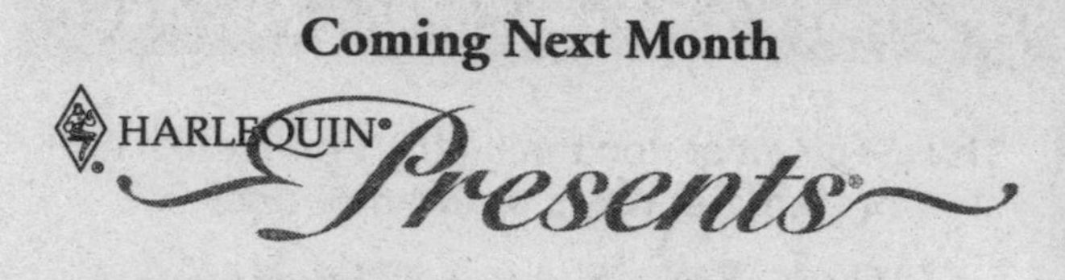

THE BEST HAS JUST GOTTEN BETTER!

#2487 THE RAMIREZ BRIDE Emma Darcy
Nick Ramirez has fame, fortune—and any girl he wants! But now he's forced to abandon his pursuit of pleasure to meet his long-lost brothers. He must find a wife and produce an heir within a year. And there's only one woman he'd choose to be the Ramirez bride....

#2488 EXPOSED: THE SHEIKH'S MISTRESS Sharon Kendrick
As the ruler of a desert kingdom, Sheikh Hashim Al Aswad must marry a respectable woman. He previously left Sienna Baker when her past was exposed—and he saw the photos to prove it! But with passion this hot, can he keep away from her...?

#2489 THE TYCOON'S TROPHY WIFE Miranda Lee
Reece knew Alanna would make the perfect trophy wife! Stunning and sophisticated, she wanted a marriage of convenience. But suddenly their life together was turned upside down when Reece discovered that his wife had a dark past....

#2490 AT THE FRENCH BARON'S BIDDING Fiona Hood-Stewart
When Natasha de Saugure was summoned to France by her grandmother, inheriting a grand estate was the last thing on her mind—but her powerful new neighbor, Baron Raoul d'Argentan, believed otherwise. His family had been feuding with Natasha's for centuries—and the Baron didn't forgive....

#2491 THE ITALIAN'S MARRIAGE DEMAND Diana Hamilton
Millionaire Ettore Severini was ready to marry until he learned that Sophie Lang was a scheming thief! Now when he sees her again, Sophie is living in poverty with a baby.... Ettore has never managed to forget her, and marriage will bring him his son, revenge and Sophie at his mercy!

#2492 THE TWELVE-MONTH MISTRESS Kate Walker
Joaquin Alcolar has a rule—never to keep a mistress for more than a year! Cassie's time is nearly up.... But then an accident leaves Joaquin with amnesia. Does this mean Cassie is back where she started—in Joaquin's bed, with the clock started once more...?

HPCNM0805